Also by Thomas Rayfiel

Split-Levels

Colony Girl

Eve in the City

Parallel Play

Parallel Play

a novel

Thomas Rayfiel

Random House Trade Paperbacks
New York

A Random House Trade Paperback Original

Copyright © 2007 by Thomas Rayfiel
Reading group guide copyright © 2007 by Random House, Inc.

Published in the United States by Random House Trade Paperbacks,
an imprint of The Random House Publishing Group,
a division of Random House, Inc., New York.

RANDOM HOUSE TRADE PAPERBACKS and colophon are
trademarks of Random House, Inc.
READER'S CIRCLE and colophon are trademarks of
Random House, Inc.

ISBN 978-0-345-45519-2

Library of Congress Cataloging-in-Publication Data
Rayfiel, Thomas
Parallel play: a novel / Thomas Rayfiel.
p.   cm.
ISBN 978-0-345-45519-2 (pbk.)
1. Motherhood—Drama.   I. Title.

PS3568.A9257P37 2007
813'.54—dc22
2006049392

Printed in the United States of America

www.thereaderscircle.com

2   4   6   8   9   7   5   3   1

Text design by Laurie Jewell

for SAR

ylb, t

Parallel Play

Chapter One

I didn't get pregnant all at once. There were several men and several times and then one morning I woke up and said, "Oh God." Believe me, I know that's not how things are supposed to happen. My life had stopped obeying the Laws of Nature. I was so busy wondering if this was it. Every touch, every feeling, became a possible big moment, until I couldn't even concentrate on enjoying myself, if that's what I was meant to be doing. I remember thinking, There has to be more, doesn't there? I still had a sense of *future* about to start, of a destiny, a calling, just for me. And then it was over, my life. I was staring at a pink dot, a period at the end of a sentence that hadn't been written yet. Over before it had begun.

"How old is your baby?"

"Jasper is fourteen months."

"Jasper! You're a big boy, aren't you, Jasper?"

We were sitting in the Tot Spot. Ann was either building a castle or digging a hole, I couldn't tell which. She didn't seem to know herself. The book lay open on my lap. I had brought it so no one would talk to me. I hated playground conversations. But what the other mothers said kept leaking in. I couldn't close my ears.

"And how old is . . . is it a girl?"

"Chloe will be one in February."

"Chloe!"

It had JOURNAL on the front and a blank page for every day of the year. At first I thought it was a novel and in a way it was. With no writing at all it was a perfect description of my life: Monday—nothing, Tuesday—nothing, Wednesday—

"Eve?"

There had to be more, didn't there? I remembered waiting for words to appear, some explanation or congratulations or even a stupid saying like in a fortune cookie. I still had the stick some-where: Accu-Preg Early Warning System. Maybe if I peed on it again. . . .

"Eve!"

He was standing on the other side of the fence. I had forgotten anyone existed beyond our closed-off little world. Though he'd called my name, twice, he still hesitated, not sure it was me. I don't know why. I recognized him right away.

"Hello, Mark."

He came closer and put his hands on the bars.

"Is that yours?"

No, I wanted to answer. I was abducted by aliens and forced to become an incubator in one of their hideous breeding experiments. Instead I just shrugged.

"Is it a boy or . . . ?"

"Girl."

"What's her name?"

"Ann."

"She's beautiful."

"Thanks."

"How old?"

"Seven months."

I was surprised at how calm I sounded. I had imagined this meeting so many times, played it over in my mind, but now that it was actually happening, seeing Mark again turned out not to be such a big deal after all. Then I realized he'd asked me another question, about a minute ago.

"What?"

"I said, Who's the lucky guy?"

"No one. I mean, his name's Harvey. Harvey Gabriel. He's a doctor."

"A doctor?"

He looked the same, as if the last two and a half years hadn't happened, which of course they hadn't, not to him. He wasn't handsome. That was his secret weapon. He looked so ordinary, under a tangle of silly white-boy dreadlocks. The way kids don't have fully formed features yet, how their faces are fresh, as if some wrapper has just been pulled back, that was Mark, even though he was twenty-four. No, twenty-seven, now. My age, still.

"What are you doing here?" I asked.

"I moved. To one of those lofts near the bridge."

Ann was licking a train that had been handled last by a child who looked like he had leprosy. I took it away from her and she began to cry.

"You mean, you *live* here?"

"For about a month now."

I hauled her into my lap. She immediately started squirming around, rooting at the buttons of my coat.

"Great," I muttered.

I could feel him watching.

"I can't believe it's you, Eve."

"Me neither."

I undid the coat and pushed up my shirt. It was cold but hadn't snowed yet. That's why we were all outside. Snow was going to be a death sentence.

"So what's happening?" he went on. "What are you up to?"

"Taking care of her, mostly."

"Does she do that a lot?"

"Do what?"

"Cry."

"All the time."

Her gums finally clamped down. I'd heard women say how much they loved nursing, how it made them feel "complete." Apparently that was another gene I was born without, along with the Mindless Chatter gene, because all it did was make me feel I'd been attacked by a giant toothless rat.

"You should come see the place." To give him credit, he wasn't pretending not to notice, the way most men did. I kind of wished he had been. Instead, he gazed down at us, making me uncomfortable. "I have it fixed up just like before."

We were quiet. There wasn't much to say. There never had been. That was both the strength and weakness of our time together.

"Listen," he began, "about what happened—"

"Ow! You little bitch!" I snapped.

He looked shocked.

I tried smiling, turning the whole thing into a joke. I just called my daughter a bitch. Ha-ha. Crazy Eve.

"Are you OK?"

"Of course I'm OK. She just bit me, that's all."

I changed sides.

All these irritating things about Mark were coming back, things I knew but had carefully layered over. For instance, the way he always dressed the same, as if weather didn't affect him. He had on a tan-and-white-checked flannel shirt I remembered intimately, that I had buried my face in a hundred times, and jeans with a hole in each knee, the same wide slit, and those lace-up boots. . . . I fell into the memory, the sound of them banging over the floor of the Greene Street loft, that suction *whoosh* they made when he took them off. It was such a complex mix of anger and attraction. Not my type, not my type, I used to repeat, clinging to that objection, the last hope of someone about to drown in love, until it got turned upside down, into a virtue. What's so great . . . is how he is not my type.

"I'm married too."

"You are." I said it as if I knew, then realized I did. He had a ring.

"No kids, though. Her name's Iolanthe."

"Of course."

I knew that too, somehow. Iolanthe was the only possible name Mark's wife could have. Mark's wife. There were two words that didn't go together.

"She's a dancer."

Now there was really nothing left to say. I almost scolded him: Here at the Tot Spot, we do not talk about marrying dancers. The fence got higher. Wind worked its way under my clothes. I was being gnawed at and frozen solid at the same time.

"You," he said, as if he just noticed, "look fantastic."

I hit this air pocket in my thoughts, bounced once, hard, then saw he meant Ann. He had that goofy stare people without children get.

"Can you believe this?" Marjorie called, parking her double stroller and plopping down next to me on the bench. She pretended not to notice Mark, which I didn't believe, since she was always commenting on men, even when they were across the street. "I mean, it's only December. So what's new?"

"Nothing."

. . . just exposing my breasts to an ex-lover. Ex-boyfriend? Old boyfriend?

Luckily, Ann was finished. I admired her drugged, open mouth. Now she would fall asleep.

"Well, hello there."

Marjorie was the kind of mother I wished I could be, very outrageous and bitchy but so on top of things. With men, she used this extreme form of flirtation. You could never tell if she was kidding. I assumed it was in reaction to what had happened (her husband left almost immediately after the twins were born), unless that was the way she'd always been. I wouldn't know. I hadn't met any mothers before they had their kid. I barely remembered myself, from back then.

"Now, do you work for the Parks Department?" she asked. "Because I have a problem with the sandbox here."

You're married? I joined in silently, trying to pick up a little of her aggression. Who gave you permission to get married?

"Just because it's winter doesn't mean the sand shouldn't be raked on a regular basis. My little Ian found a frozen dog turd the other day."

"Marjorie—"

"I mean what are you guys doing from nine to five?" Her eyes did this X-ray thing over his chest. "Besides lifting weights, apparently."

"This is my friend Mark."

"Oh!" It was all a joke, to make up for the big joke played on her. "So you're not here to rake the sandbox? Because you look like you'd be really good at it. Maybe you'd have to take off some more of your clothes, but—"

"Mark's a carpenter."

"Contractor," he corrected.

I frowned. That was new.

"What, like buildings and stuff?" Marjorie asked.

"Interior design. Private residences. I work with architects now," he said, implying he'd moved up in the world, that I didn't know him anymore.

Just then Alex, or maybe Ian, I could never tell them apart, woke up. While Marjorie was dealing with him, Mark leaned closer and said, "I'm sorry."

"About what?"

"You know."

I honestly didn't. Then he gave me this look, as if he'd unloaded some burden by apologizing. He shivered, hugged himself, and stamped his feet. It destroyed the last of my illusions. In my mind he had stayed untouched by anything, guilt or cold or status. But now it turned out he was just like everyone else, standing there saying he was a contractor instead of a carpenter, trying to stay warm, apologizing for our past.

"So listen, if you guys were having a private conversation—"

"No!"

I blushed at the urgency in my voice, how badly I wanted him to go away. He was embarrassing.

"Hey, we should all get together," he said. "The four of us."

"That would be *great*," I answered, with the enthusiasm of telling a pure lie. "I'll call you."

I'll look you up in the yellow pages, under Asshole.

"It's just amazing, seeing you again, Eve."

I had so much distance on him now. I could hear how he made his voice deepen, become husky, see how, before turning, he gave a shy apologetic smile, how he shrugged as if to say he was not responsible. That was Mark. Not responsible for how he made you feel, shrugging beautiful shoulders.

Marjorie cast a lingering, unashamed gaze as he hiked up the hill into the park. His dreadlocks bounced at each step. He had a red bandanna hooked through a belt loop. It hung down and wagged.

"He's going to run."

I don't know why it sounded so revealing. Just that I knew his routine.

"Poor thing." Ian, or maybe Alex, was whimpering. She jogged him on her knee. "Is Poopsie sad because the big strong bodybuilder man went away?"

"Shut up."

"Annie's mommy is a wee bit cranky this afternoon."

"I am not."

"She's imagining what life would be like without children."

Marjorie was the only other mother who understood. The rest of them pretended to complain, but meanwhile they were just glowing with barely concealed pride, in—what? That's what I always wanted to ask. In having this greedy sucking puking pissing shitting *thing* practically attached to you for the next ten years? "You just haven't bonded yet." They smiled wisely, early on, when I was still stupid enough to say what I felt. Then, after a while, they didn't say anything. I ranted on and on into a void. Finally, by mutual agreement, we stopped sitting together. I would look for a bench at the far end of the Tot Spot, under the trees, where sand collected and mixed with acorns, blown leaves, and dirt to form a stinking mulch. That's where Marjorie camped out with her behemoth of a stroller. She had gotten so big, just in the time since we first met, as if there needed to be more of her, to cope.

"How can he run in those shoes?"

He was on the ring road now and had broken into a trot.

"He does everything in them."

We both stared. He moved so comfortably, a big cat, a male lion, the kind who just basks in the sun or slouches through tall grass. Being with Mark was like watching a nature film.

"Well, almost everything, right?"

I didn't answer. He disappeared behind some trees. As soon as he was gone, I came back down to earth.

"Dammit to hell!"

That was another reaction to parenthood nobody else seemed to have, that none of the books mentioned. I swore a lot. Words came out of my mouth, sometimes ordinary cursing, other times bizarre, shocking combinations.

"What?"

"She's wet."

"Sure it's not you?"

Marjorie took out a plastic bag of teething biscuits. I got down on my hands and knees. Of course I didn't have a clean white piece of cloth, the way everyone else did so they could create a sterile operating-room-theater environment. Instead, Ann thrashed around in the sand-dirt-wood-grub mixture that people said carried West Nile virus, wailing like a police car siren while I peeled off the bloated diaper with one hand and kept her legs trussed with the other.

"Lie still," I said patiently.

"I had a boyfriend like that once." Marjorie broke a biscuit in half and ate it herself. "He played the drums."

"He was not my boyfriend."

I put a finger between Ann's feet so her two little ankle bones wouldn't rub together (you did so much on automatic pilot, assimilated so many details) and tried dabbing away at the raw skin. She had an endless case of diaper rash. You'd think she would have been grateful for the cold air hitting it, drying it out, but her screams only rose higher, to the treetops.

"Stop crying." I tried to confuse her by sounding concerned when I was really just furious. I squirted medicated talc on her chubby thighs. "Wait until something bad happens before you cry."

"Brice," she remembered. "Isn't that a beautiful name? Or maybe it was Tony. Anyway, he showed up when Sherman and I were on our honeymoon. That was awkward. He was the chef at a restaurant we went to. He came out of the kitchen to say hello."

"I thought you said he played the drums."

"He did. At night."

Boyfriend. Ex-lover. They were such ridiculous terms. Mark wasn't any of those. He was a whole choppy period in my life, the embodiment of all that was going on then. I didn't blame him for what happened. I always felt I was using Mark to make myself miserable, maneuvering him into place to torture me. That's what made me mad when he apologized, that he thought he'd had power over me.

"It just pisses me off!"

I stopped. I had forgotten what I was going to say.

"Him showing up here and acting like nothing's changed?"

"No. It's not about Mark. I told you, he's not that big a deal."

"You're just suddenly in a bad mood for no reason?"

"Exactly."

Concentrating, I finished changing Ann and sat back down.

We put the children side by side. Each acted like the other didn't exist, was in another dimension or part of nature, a force that stopped a leg from moving, caused a toy to vanish. "Parallel play." It was supposed to be good for them, although I didn't see how. There were whole groups devoted to it, signs up on the playground's metal gate, now that the weather was getting bad. PARALLEL PLAY GROUP THURSDAYS 9:30–11. QUESTIONS? CALL JANICE.

Ann tried to sit up. She leaned forward on one hand and balanced.

"Oh, she's tripoding," another mother cooed, passing by.

"Mind your own cocksucking business."

Had I really said that? I checked my lips. No. They were still pressed together, holding the words inside. But just barely.

"I remember!"

"Remember what?"

"What I was mad about."

"Oh. Well, *that's* good."

"Look." I showed her the journal. "Harvey gave me this."

She fanned through the pages. I hadn't written anything yet.

"What for?"

"I have no idea. Don't you think that's weird?"

"Why?"

"I mean, we're barely speaking to each other, and his solution is to give me a blank book?"

"Harvey seems like a nice guy."

"He is." I made it sound like the last nail in the coffin of our marriage. "Very nice."

"At least he's not running around with a woman half his age who tells people she works in product branding."

"What is that, anyway?"

"It has something to do with advertising. I think she hands out free samples. At least Sherman thought they were free. I'm sure he's finding out differently now. No hitting, Alex."

Marjorie's life had been far more completely wrecked than mine. She used to be a lawyer. She didn't seem to mind what had happened, though. I mean, she admitted what a horrible time she was having, what a rotten deal it was that Sherman had left, but she wasn't losing it. Not like me. Maybe it helped that she was older, in her forties, and always wanted kids. Of all the regulars at the Tot Spot, we were probably at the two extremes, in terms of age.

"Are you leaving for the holidays?" she asked.

"No, I don't think so. Why?"

"Will you water my plants? And take in the mail? It's only for a week. We'll be upstate with my mother."

"Sure. No problem."

"Are you celebrating Christmas or Hanukkah? Or both?"

"Celebrate?"

She looked at me funny, took out another teething biscuit, and picked up the book again, as if an entry might have appeared since the last time.

"I think it's nice Harvey gave you this. You should write something in it."

I laughed, thinking she was joking, but an hour later, alone again, found a pencil and opened the journal to the first page. I held the point right over the paper and waited for something to happen. Of course nothing did. Finally, I just made some marks, scratches, what a chimp would do or, worse, a child.

* * *

After the playground we went uphill, into the park. I loved the Long Meadow. It stretched so far your eyes unkinked their muscles, found resting spots—a grove of trees, a pond, the rise of a hill—then continued their journey until they got lost in their own perception. A yawn welled up and wiped out all your anxieties, expelled dirt and poison from your thoughts, so when you looked again you saw the world whole and fresh. You checked back in with some primal sanity.

That's what I had come to expect, but when I got to the top of the path, yellow tape was wound across two trees, the kind the police use when marking off an accident or crime scene.

"What's going on?" I asked.

No one else was around. There weren't many people, this time of year. It had been cold for so long the rock-hard ground and scraped pavement looked raw, as if snow would be a blessing. Still, I was there to walk and didn't see why anyone should stop me. You couldn't close off such a big space. That was part of its beauty. I lifted the tape and ducked under.

I was so tired I didn't even see the cables until I pushed the stroller right over them. Ann, who had just recovered from the changing incident, started to whimper all over again at being bumped.

"Oh, sweetheart."

I was too exhausted to be angry. I parked us by a bench and rocked her in my arms. You slid from one emotion to the next. Colors, I thought drowsily. Your world was red, then green, then blue, like someone was turning a knob, a giant, unseen Hand. I sniffed back tears. The slats of the bench were leaving a pattern.

"We are losing the light," a voice complained. "And if we lose the light, we lose all."

You're hearing things, I told myself. First seeing colors, now hearing voices. But it was a strange voice to imagine because it had an English accent.

Someone else spoke. I couldn't make out what he said but heard the same voice answer.

"Doing it artificially never looks right. Besides, it is about to clear up. She is still a young girl, you see, despite all that has happened to her. All she needs now is a ray of pure sunshine on her features; then she will be saved. That, ultimately, is what we are after. Salvation."

I turned. Twenty people were behind me, a few yards off, in a place that, a moment ago, had been completely empty. A whole world appeared where the cables led, I saw now, with big lights on stands, wagons of what looked like pipe, boards of electronic equipment, and a card table set up with food. In the middle of it, a tiny man, very round and short, clearly the center of attention, watched all the activity going on around him. He was balding, with a small nose, sharp eyes, and hands sunk deep in the pockets of a beautiful green overcoat. The rest of the film crew were younger, regular-sized and casual-looking, wearing leather bomber jackets or down vests. They were all in motion, carrying out orders. He was perfectly still, the one in charge. You could tell. Even though he had the voice of a child.

"Is everyone ready?" he asked, with just a hint of exasperation. "Is *anyone* ready?"

By this point, I was twisted completely around. The director moved off to look at something and all of them followed. He was the sliding knot of the group's attention.

Meanwhile, Ann's unhappiness had turned to tears. Not your garden variety boo-hoo-I'm-sad crying, more like she had just discovered the world had no meaning, a real existentialist-despair meltdown, which I ignored because it was nothing unusual. It happened two or three times a day.

"Shush," I said distractedly.

"People," the little man called, clapping his hands, "if each could just concentrate on his or her appointed task. There is a method to my madness, I assure you."

Portable heaters made a rippling wall of air so it was hard to follow his progress, to see past the border into the enchanted kingdom where he ruled. I blinked, trying to focus not just my eyes but my attention.

"No, no, no, my dear. You must be surprised by Grace, not act as if it were some tuxedo-clad escort, late in arriving. Here. Stand like this."

There was a girl, waiting for him. I couldn't see her that well but she didn't seem particularly pretty. Her face was slightly bigger than normal, as if it had been magnified by all the attention placed on it. He started touching her, moving her body around, shaping it. The way he handled her was completely impersonal, not in a mean way, just the essence of unsexual, which I found weirdly attractive. The whole time, he was talking to her, pouring words directly into her ear, but of course I couldn't hear what, even though I was straining forward.

"There." He stood back to admire his work. "Now all we need is a little cooperation from the sky."

He gestured like a magician, and all of us—the people clustered around him, the actress standing in her unnatural position, me sitting on my bench—looked up to see the sun break free from a last shred of cloud.

A shaft of light drenched the girl in liquid gold.

My heart leaped.

"Places!" another person yelled.

The whole time, I had been using a set of long-dead muscles, dead so long I had forgotten what they were used *for*. Now it came back, as I felt them stir to life. I was willing him to notice me, that pathetic stare you put on someone that never works and only later you realize makes you look like a total idiot. But I couldn't help it. For some reason I needed this stranger's recognition the way your body decides it needs a certain vitamin or mineral. It was crucial to my health, to my mental well-being, and amazingly, miraculously, I got it. In the middle of the finely tuned chaos going on around him, he turned, drawn by my enormous all-consuming hunger. Cutting through the intervening fuzziness, not just the hot air of the heaters, the stubbly cheeks of all the would-be men, but through my own half-baked thoughts, my mixed-up wants and fears, he gazed directly into my eyes. It was a moment of utter connection.

"Jonathon!" he called.

The way he spoke was beautiful, so precise. Each word was a jewel. Each syllable was a facet on that jewel.

A man with a clipboard trotted over to see what was wrong.

He was still staring at me as he gave orders to the assistant, who nodded once and took off again, walking toward me fast, saying, "Ma'am?"

He was summoning me, through his helper. I didn't know for what. It didn't really matter. I hadn't thought that far ahead. Just the fact that the look had worked, that he had noticed me, sensed my worth. I was still stuck back on that.

"Ma'am, this is a reserved area."

The assistant was holding up his hands as he approached, shielding the scene from my prying eyes.

"Hi!" I said stupidly.

"We have a permit to film here. Didn't you see the tape?"

"Me?" I asked, playing for time.

"We're trying to shoot a scene, and your child is making so much noise that—"

Other members of the group were staring too—not at me, I realized now, but at Ann. Even by her standards, she was having a classic fit. I was just so used to these displays that my response was to space out, which I guess was what I'd been doing, twisted around on the bench, picking some faraway object almost at random, in this case a fiftyish five-foot-short Englishman, and then concentrating on him, investing him with all kinds of phony significance, to take my mind off—well, my life. The alternative was to jam a dirty saliva-soaked Mickey Mouse mitten down her throat, so really I was doing us both a favor, but I could see how, from the outside, it must have made me look like the ultimate uncaring mother.

"I'm sorry." I woke slowly, painfully, out of a dream. "I didn't realize."

"If you could just take your child away now? Because we have a very short window of time to work in."

Then I heard the voice again, except this time it wasn't enunciating words of wisdom that mysteriously applied to my personal problems. Instead it had a neighing, braying quality, forcing you to listen.

"—simply must do a better job of sealing off the perimeter. I cannot continue to work when you allow the presence of screaming infants to interfere with my cinematography. Now if we could hurry and *refocus,* people, before—"

I got her into the stroller. She fought me every step of the way. I had to use brute strength, which I hated, forcing her little arms back.

"She's colicky," I tried explaining, "which you'd think was a real medical term but turns out to be a catchall word for a kid who screams nonstop and turns your life into a living hell."

"Great," the man with the clipboard answered, not listening.

"That's why I didn't realize what was going on. What you were doing. I was just resting here, and then I must have nodded off, because—"

As soon as I got the last plastic buckle to click in place, she began arching her back and keening like a patient in a mental hospital.

"Shut up!" I hissed.

The assistant lifted the tape. I had to bend low to pass under. It wasn't until we were halfway home that I saw why I had gotten so mad.

"Ma'am," I remembered, glaring down at Ann. "He called me ma'am."

• • •

Brooklyn wasn't Manhattan. There was no sense of mystery, no answer waiting just around the corner. Things didn't happen for a reason, at least none I could see. They just piled up, a jumble of events. Of course it was me, my life, getting married and having a child, that caused this despair, not moving to a different part of the city. That's what I told myself. It wouldn't matter where I lived, under these circumstances. Still, I did feel I had taken a wrong turn. Every other place I'd lived in seemed so . . . biblical, as if the theology of my life was being acted out there. But now, whatever was due to happen had already come and gone. I was just another yawning, stupid member of the crowd, pushing home my daughter.

During the day, Seventh Avenue had the feeling of a village. You saw the same faces. The street was lined with shops: an ancient hardware store, dark and packed with tools, or the butcher's, where I went now, with a sawdust-sprinkled floor and five or six guys behind the counter, all in bloodstained white aprons. There was a wooden chair on the customer side of the glass case, for neighborhood women to sit in and gossip with the owner. This time an Italian widow was there, dressed in black, as I squeezed the stroller past.

"Mother," he said, "what can I do for you?"

I didn't know why I came. There was a supermarket one block closer that had ground beef wrapped in plastic. Here, you were a target the minute you walked in. Or else they ignored you completely. But I had a craving for meat. It was left over from my pregnancy. Something about the oozing displays fascinated me, made me salivate. Maybe how repulsive they were.

"I got a nice pork chop."

"Wait, I have a recipe."

"She has a recipe!"

He had white hair, a lot of it, brushed back and stiffened with some ancient cream.

"It's here somewhere."

I fumbled for it in my pocket, coming out with a balled-up twenty-dollar bill, a pacifier, and a perfectly preserved Band-Aid. I could see, for the first time, the reason behind having a big ugly handbag. Before, I had always thought it was to hit attackers over the head with.

"Are you a good girl?" he was asking Ann, while I searched some more. "Are you good to your mother?"

"Here." I smoothed it out and tried remembering why I wanted to make this in the first place.

"What do you need, dear?"

"Beef tenderloin," I read. With blue cheese sauce? It sounded disgusting.

"Filet mignon," he told one of his assistants, who disappeared into the back. "How much? A pound?"

"Three pounds."

"No, no, no. You throwing a party?"

The terrified look in my eyes told him I wasn't.

"You want a pound. This stuff is like butter."

I looked at the recipe again. Sure enough, it was for A Classic New Year's Eve: Serves Eight. What was I thinking?

"I'm going to make it nice for you." He took his knife and starting mincing away at the fat. "You stick this in the oven, put on a dress, some perfume . . ."

He started humming. I watched the blade, with tiny movements, make all the white streaks, the bluish membrane, fall away, until there was nothing left but a cylinder of red.

"You feeling all right?" he asked. "You look a little tired."

"I'm fine."

"Got to keep your strength up. You know what they say."

I waited for him to tell me.

"It's a good life, if you don't weaken."

It was more expensive than I thought. I tried not to act surprised. Harvey wouldn't mind. Besides, it was worth it. I was paying for human contact, which I liked, the paying part. I tipped up the wheels to get past the lady in the chair. Her swollen elephant legs, with orthopedic stockings bunched up at the ankles, stuck out into the narrow aisle. She reached into the stroller—I hated it when people did that—and pinched Ann's cheek.

"Cute," she grunted.

We lived downhill from Seventh, in an apartment building, not on one of the brownstone blocks near the park. Harvey wasn't sure if the neighborhood was a good place to raise a child. "Since when do we let her dictate our actions?" I asked, which must have sounded funny, since at the time she was pretty much all I was using as a guide. What did she want? What did she need? I saw the appeal, the seduction, of being a mother. You could just give up all your hopes and dreams, heap them on your kid. Devote yourself to her. It was so acceptable. Even though there were women on TV being police officers and presidents of companies, the real world you met day after day was full of encouragement to stop wanting for yourself and want, instead, for your child. Harvey felt none of this. Having Ann just made him more determined to succeed, to get ahead, to provide. He was big on that.

"It's only for a few years," everyone said.

I held her in one hand, collapsing and snapping shut the stroller with the other, using my foot and the wall while shouldering open the door and somehow snagging my keys. I kept having these hallucinations I had grown another limb, an extra appendage.

It annoyed me. Having a child appealed to Harvey's strengths, inspired him, while for me it just tempted my weaknesses, to weep and give up. I cried all the time now, for no reason, looking at a leaf or smelling fresh bread. I was so fragile.

"A Classic New Year's Eve," I announced, using my butt—which was threatening to become my real new appendage if I wasn't careful—to slam the door and barricade it.

It was only early December, but I was counting so much on the New Year to solve all our problems that I wanted to try out the meal in advance.

The place was still a complete pigsty. I kept having these fantasies someone would break in while we were away, pick up all the toys, vacuum, do the dishes, scrub the toilet, then leave.

"You know, like a Dirt Thief," I had tried explaining that morning.

"It's called a cleaning lady," Harvey answered. "Carmelita."

"Who?"

"That's the woman we had, growing up. I could ask around, see if anyone knows—"

"No."

"You just said how much you wanted someone to come in."

"I did not. I'm not getting a cleaning lady. Who do you think I am? What are you trying to turn me into?"

"So do it yourself. It isn't that hard. What do you do the whole time she's asleep, anyway?"

That was another reason I wanted us to have a nice meal, to make up for the pillow I threw at him right before he left. I hadn't meant to break his glasses. It must have hit just right. Now it was getting dark and, despite all my good intentions, I hadn't accomplished a thing.

I slung her down on the futon, the one piece of furniture from my old apartment, coaxed her out of her jacket, sweater, mittens, and shoes. She took so long between breaths. Her whole body stopped, then gathered itself. What do they dream about, I wondered, with such little material to work with?

Hardly any memories. Hardly any emotions either, compared to later. I watched her and waited for the valve in my chest to open. Slowly, it loosened. I allowed myself to feel. It was the vulnerability, her delicate eyelids, or maybe our being alone.

This is what I do while she sleeps, I answered, defending myself. I practice loving her, but only in private, where no one can see.

Of course what you really had to do while they slept was crash out yourself. You had to mimic their rhythms. It was the only way to stay sane. Instead, I "thoroughly oiled" the meat and "cut it into medallions." I chopped, diced, grated, and peeled. I stooped to grab all the plastic toys and fluffy stuffed animals. There was no place to put anything. She didn't have her own room yet. We hadn't thought that far ahead. There was the living room, with the futon, some chairs, the table where we ate, and then, through a large opening, another space, where her crib and the changing table were set up. Her things spread to every surface. All I could do was arrange them in artistic-looking piles. Mounds of teddy bears, dogs, sheep, even a lobster. A whole corner of rattles, teething rings, and balls. Then I remembered the butcher's advice, took a shower, and put on a dress. Why not? I didn't have any perfume, so I smeared a few drops of Harvey's Pour l'Homme cologne behind each ear to confuse him, or to confuse myself.

We hadn't made love in eight months.

I stared at the mirror and thought, This is how you looked a minute ago. You're seeing into the past when you look at your reflection, light from a distant star. I was someone else now, not this person with too-long hair and a surprised wide-eyed expression, the pre-motherhood Eve. "Harvey's child bride," I heard his friend Mindy say, when she thought I was out of the room.

The girl peering back at me over the sink was just that, a girl. I was flooded with weepy regret, not for anything in particular, just a nameless formless longing looking to attach itself to whatever came along.

It wasn't until Ann was born that I did the math and figured out I'd had her at the exact same age my mother had me. That was depressing. It made me feel I was on a sled, going downhill. Sure, I could lean a little from side to side and maybe influence where I went, to the right a few feet or to the left, give it my own personal style, but basically my future was already decided. I was doomed to whiz by and disappear, just like the person before me. Which made me wonder if there was really any "me" at all, or if we were just caught in some loop, repeating mistakes we called accidents but were really our defining characteristics, who we were.

I reread the recipe. Cooking was hard. I interpreted too much, started imagining instructions that weren't there. "Boil until liquid is thick enough to coat a spoon." What did that really mean? It seemed so open-ended. But this time everything went right. I was on my way, rolling along, until I noticed the telephone message light flashing. It was Harvey, calling while I was in the shower, saying he'd be late, not home before eleven. The meat was already on. I had been about to "tent it loosely with foil," so we could sit down, have a drink, talk . . .

Did I mention we hadn't made love in eight months?

It was my fault, of course. When I was in labor, she wouldn't come out right away so they decided to use forceps. I caught a glimpse, even though I wasn't supposed to ("Don't look!" they kept saying), but it was so distorted in my memory I refused to believe what I saw: curved steel grippers, a giant gleaming scoop. I didn't feel anything at the time, but after, when the pills wore off, I was so swollen I could barely move. There was an invisible bolster between my legs. That had gone away a long time ago, but by then other things started happening, like our both passing out at night from exhaustion, never being alone, fighting, and just being repulsed, I think, by anything having to do with the body. We were dealing with all this aftermath, the wreckage of our former happiness, which the world kept stubbornly insisting was really a beginning, a new life.

I listened to the message again. The hospital paging system blared in the background. He didn't sound mad at me. Ann was up by now, so I put her in the swing. I only allowed myself two windups most nights because she looked a little sick when she was doing it. Her head flopped, always a second behind her body, causing cases of mini-whiplash. But she liked it. It sent her into a trance. I poured myself a glass of wine and ate some meat without the sauce or the asparagus or even the plate, just stood over the pan with a forkful of semi-raw cow. A medallion. It tasted good. I surveyed my situation. Another cozy evening at home. How could I club these next few hours to death?

Mark wasn't in the phone book. Of course not. He said he had only moved a month ago. Then I remembered how his old number was a big secret. He wouldn't write it down. You weren't supposed to either. You had to memorize it. He was paranoid about the police, except in his case, considering how he really made his money (not by "contracting," like he had told Marjorie), it wasn't paranoia. I would probably never see him again, which was fine with me. I wasn't really going to call. I was just curious. Curious to see what his new number looked like. The shape of it. Ann slowed down and stared. She knew what I'd been up to.

"Daddy's going to be a little late," I said.

My voice sounded deeper than usual, and thick. Thick enough to coat a spoon.

"Talk to her more," everyone urged. "That's how she learns, by listening to you. Talk to her all the time."

But I couldn't. In the park, on the street, in coffee shops, all I heard was mothers keeping up this running commentary. "Mommy's going to pick you up now. Here we go. Up in the air! You're getting so big. How did you get so big? Isn't today a beautiful day? Look how blue the sky is." Maybe it was because I never played with dolls, but I found it awkward and unnatural.

"I talk to her when I have something to say," I answered.

They looked startled, like I was some kind of monster.

Instead, I wanted someone to talk to *me*. Was that too much to ask for? I was tired of initiating conversations with, if you could take away the insulting sound of it, a complete moron. I was drinking a second glass of wine now, and I'd finished half the meat. I put everything away, quickly, without looking, as if it was about to attack me. Mugged by a filet mignon.

You're doing fine, I told myself. The place is clean, dinner's waiting (he usually got something at the hospital, but just in case), the kid's alive. What more could anyone ask?

I don't know how we got through the rest of the evening. The same way we'd gotten through a hundred others. I read a book to her that she didn't understand, bathed her while she screamed so loud the sound split my eardrums, did another windup, fell asleep, and woke just a minute later totally disoriented, not knowing where I was, with the suspicion she'd been watching me, that a tiny part of her life had gone on without my knowledge. Finally I got her to bed, lowering her into the crib with my arms stretching and my back aching. Then I sang, the one part of the job I didn't mind, not lullabies or psalms but "The Star-Spangled Banner."

"Oh, say can you see—"

It was the only song I remembered the words to.

"—by the dawn's early light . . ."

Chapter Two

We met at a free clinic. He was the doctor, I was the patient.

"I don't see a last name here," he frowned, going over the card I'd filled out.

"No last names in the Bible."

"What?"

"Nothing. I don't believe in last names, that's all."

He knelt down to look at my foot. His scalp was just beginning to show.

By then, I had developed this defense mechanism and saw, in any man who caused even the slightest spark, the paunchy middle-aged troll he would soon become. It was a way of neutralizing my desires, protecting myself against hurt. I was very proud of this discovery.

"Just because you don't believe in a thing doesn't stop it from existing."

"What do you mean?"

"Everyone has a last name. Whether they believe in last names or not."

Now I wouldn't be blinded by looks or attitude or any other superficial trait. Instead—I followed the argument to its logical conclusion—I'd end up with a man I wasn't attracted to at all. Which wasn't my aim, of course. It was just a way I'd found to take a temporary break.

"Women don't, actually."

"Don't what?"

"Have last names. Take me, for instance. I'm just Eve."

He was only half listening, making mindless conversation, working on his bedside manner.

"Well, just Eve, I'm Dr. Gabriel. Does this hurt?" He flexed my ankle, very gently.

I shook my head. I was in agony and for some reason didn't want him to know.

"What about this?"

"Excuse me, but are you a real doctor?"

He looked up.

"I mean, you seem a little young. Not young exactly, but . . ."

"What would you call a real doctor?"

"Someone who knows what he's doing?"

He nodded, like that was one possible answer.

"In that sense, yes. I know what I'm doing. Don't you?"

"Well, not consciously."

He stopped for a minute, then went back to examining my foot.

"I'm sorry." I tried again. "It's just that you seem closer to my age, and I'm used to doctors who are old. Not old, but *older*. I guess it's me, really, not being young anymore. I mean it's not like I'm forty-five or anything, but—"

"Actually, you're right."

"I am? About what?"

"I got my medical license three weeks ago. I do know what I'm doing, but I'm not sure that makes me a real doctor yet."

"Oh."

"This is my first rotation, working here at the clinic."

"I thought so."

"How could you tell?"

"I don't know. You seem . . ." My voice trailed off.

The problem was, once I started looking at men that way, it became almost impossible to stop. I saw the bald spot in every full head of hair, mentally inflated the thirty-pound inner tube belted around each man's waist. But Harvey was already so grown up, so serious and intense, handling my foot like it was some kind of complex puzzle, turning it in all different directions. With him, the process was reversed. Even though he was solid, with a broad, handsome adult face, I saw back into his youth, to the lonely child.

He was touching my toes now, wiggling them one by one. This little piggy went to market. This little piggy stayed home. This little piggy had roast beef. This little piggy had none. A bolt of pain shot through me.

And this little piggy, this little piggy—

"You're not telling," he complained.

"Telling what?"

"When it hurts."

I wasn't interested in him. How could I be? He was a doctor. Even if he was only a few years older, he was already prepared to enter a different stage of life. That was obvious. Although what that stage was, I didn't know. I couldn't imagine. The mysterious next.

"Just Eve?" he repeated, finally hearing what I'd said ten minutes ago.

"Never mind."

"No, I'm curious. What did you mean?"

"I was raised in a place where we didn't have last names."

"What kind of place was that?"

"A religious colony in the middle of Iowa. We lived our lives based on Scripture." I was pronouncing each word with a weird intensity but felt I had to go on talking, to conceal the fact that I was about to pass out. My foot was on fire. "I'm a Tertiary Baptist, or was, so a lot of stuff here is still new to me. Like last names. There are no last names in the Bible."

"But—"

"I mean, women change their names all the time, when they get married."

Great, I thought. Why don't you just propose to the guy?

His hand traced an invisible line up my ankle.

"But even with men"—I swallowed, trying to obliterate that last remark—"it's just the name of your father's father's father. Back forever."

"In my case, it isn't even that. Gabriel is a middle name. My great-grandfather, when he came over, at Ellis Island, only got as far as 'Chaim Gavriel—' before they cut him off and yelled, 'Next!' He never got to say what his real last name was. At least that's the family legend."

"So who was he, really?"

"Nobody knows. He wouldn't tell. He took it as an omen. A new start."

"Ow!"

He stood up and started writing on a prescription pad.

I stared at him. "So you don't have one either."

"Your toe is fractured."

"A last name," I persisted. "Same as me."

"I guess you're right, I'm just Harvey." He tore off the sheet. "Unfortunately, there's not much you can do. These are pills, for the pain. You're going to have to stay off it for a few days."

"I can't. I'm working."

He shook his head.

"No work. Bed rest, with the foot elevated. Did someone come with you? You should take a taxi home."

"A taxi? You think if I could pay for a taxi I'd come here in the first place?"

"Good point. You'd go to a real doctor."

I slid off the examining table and almost fell. It throbbed a lot worse now that I knew something was wrong. Before, I had taken comfort in thinking the pain was all in my head. He was taller. Being high up had given me the wrong idea of our relative sizes. He caught me with one hand.

"How did you hurt yourself?"

"I didn't," I complained. "I was just walking along and then—"

"That's how it happens, sometimes."

Oh, and how would you know? I wanted to ask. Just because you're a doctor doesn't make you wise.

Clearly nothing bad had ever happened to him. I leaned hard against his side, trying to tip him over.

"Is everything all right?" he asked.

"I just want to go home."

He stopped holding me up. I couldn't blame him. I was acting obnoxious. I was so angry. I couldn't believe I had hurt myself, that it was my fault, that there was no one to blame. It seemed a sign, somehow, of how my life was going, one huge accident. I made my way out, holding on to chair backs and the wall. I could feel him behind me, that annoying magnetic presence doctors have, even three-week-old doctors like this one.

"Who's next?" he asked.

"Quack," I muttered, dragging myself through the door, out onto the street.

The next day he showed up with food.

"You can't tell anyone about this," he warned. "I could get in real trouble."

I was still so slow on the uptake I thought it was some kind of follow-up visit. A house call.

"Trouble for what? It's so nice of you."

"Copying your address, for starters. Let me see. Why isn't the leg elevated?"

Why didn't you take a bath? I was silently screaming to myself. Or at least clean the apartment?

"So this is what you do?"

I had never realized how sensitive my foot was. Not because of nerve endings. The opposite. Because it was tough and ignored, because nobody ever bothered to touch it, and now he was back to fingering it so intelligently, focusing all this expertise, reminding me it had parts: the heel, the sole, the arch.

"I do fashion knockoffs."

My voice sounded ridiculously breathy.

He nodded, indicating he'd seen the sewing machine and the tailor's dummy, all the material.

"Is that like copies?"

"Mostly high-end stuff. People see something they like, ask me to go look at it, and then . . . Am I going to be OK?"

It occurred to me he had come because I was going to lose my toe. It had turned orange-black overnight and was the size and shape of a cocktail frank. I knew it. He was a messenger of doom—

"Knockoffs. Can you make a living at that?"

—here to announce my horrible fate. But at the same time, I was still excited that he was this very professional new-style doctor, only a year or two older, who carried around with him, instead of a black bag, Chinese food.

"Barely. That's why I can't afford to stop working. I've got to make my rent. I'm worried about the nail. Is it going to fall off?" I felt myself collapsing. No one had been nice to me in so long. I didn't know how to handle it. "Please be honest. Is there anything you can do, or is the situation just completely hopeless?"

He smiled. "What did you have in mind?"

"I don't know. You're the doctor."

"So *now* I'm a doctor?"

I wasn't crying. There was just a general mistiness invading my nose and eyes.

"If there's no cure, maybe you can at least give me something to make it feel better?"

He thought for a minute, staring at the toe, then bent lower and kissed it.

"Oh."

He opened a carton. The smell of Spicy Szechuan Chicken with Cashews flooded the room.

In a way it was good, because we had gotten so much of the awkward stuff, talking, touching, out of the way early, before we even began. And in a way it wasn't, because that's where so much romance takes place, in all the early doubt. With Harvey, I somehow knew what it would be like, right from the start. There were no fantasies to be imagined, but also none to be betrayed. He was this *fact,* this meteorite that had landed in the middle of everything.

"Know what I like about you?" he said.

"What?"

I had a dread of being praised. As soon as you heard what someone liked about you, you had to keep it up, and it was usually a quality you didn't even think you had in the first place. It was usually a request to act differently, a criticism disguised as a compliment. What's he going to like about me that I'm going to be constantly trying to live up to? I wondered.

"I like how your name is the same backwards as forwards: Eve."

All right, I thought. I can live with this. It didn't seem to require too radical an adjustment.

I loved him, by an act of will. I decided to love him, and it was the best decision I ever made. But that's not to say it wasn't hard, and lately it had gotten so much harder.

Ann, on the other hand, was not a decision I made. But I still blamed myself for her. I felt, like with everything else, it was my fault, because I knew what we could and couldn't do, how far we could go, in a way he didn't. That was my one freakish and most of the time useless talent. I could make him lose control. It was just bad luck, I told myself, but how accidental could it really be if almost the first time we did it resulted in an event the rest of my body had been so busy preparing for?

He took it the same way he took everything else, very calmly and logically.

"There's a saying surgeons have when the unexpected occurs: Repair the damage and move on."

"That's easy for you to say."

"It is *not* easy for me to—" He stopped. "I'm giving you an out."

"I know you are," I said miserably.

"But if you're asking if we should do this, I vote yes."

Why did I have her? Maybe because he once told me—this was the most important thing he ever said, although he never knew it—that sex for him was the physical enactment of our relationship. I'd never thought of it that way, that it was symbolic, that we were participating in a ritual, and if we did it right, if it was good, then the rest of what we had was good too, and we could even change things, improve them, by our actions. I'm not sure I believed it, but at least it gave me a way to see, a context, because before sex had always seemed pretty senseless. Things led up to it—speed, exhilaration, fear—and things led away from it—relief, confusion, more fear—but sex itself stayed unknowable. He made it sound like a religious practice, and I understood about those. It also moved me that he was so optimistic, that he thought we, as a couple, had *meaning*.

. . .

He got home around one. I woke to the sound of his key. Footsteps creaked over the floor. I closed my eyes again. The footsteps went away, checking on Ann, then came down the hall. The door was only half closed, but when he came in it was like a seal had been broken. I could feel the cold air he brought with him from across the room.

"Hi," he said quietly, testing to see if I was up.

"Did you eat?"

"I ate."

He got into bed. Our legs bumped against each other, clumsy, clunking things.

"Sorry about your glasses."

"It's all right. They're fixed. I never thought a pillow could—"

"What happened at work?"

"Nothing. I had to make sure someone was all right."

"Were they?"

He reached across.

He didn't like to talk about what happened at the hospital. It was technical, I assumed, or confidential, or maybe I was the antidote to it all, the sweetness and light he came home to, the one who made him forget his troubles. The wife.

"How's Ann?"

"Good."

His hands smelled of antibacterial soap. He'd been up to his elbows in misery all night, then scrubbed it away, taking off a layer of skin too. My stomach knotted up. It was as if he was still wearing rubber gloves. The problem was no longer physical, a fear of pain, it was more a lack of concentration. When did making love stop being new and become a reference to all that had happened before? My mind would get distracted, lose itself in long-ago moments. When did every touch become "remember this?" We never kissed on the lips anymore. It was one memory neither of us wanted to disturb. I tried responding, and that, of all things, made him stop. He froze, in the middle of a caress. He was somewhere else too. We both were.

"What?" I asked.

"Tell me about your day."

"Oh, please."

I rolled away. My back was to him, but at the same time

I ached for him to take me. Take charge. Relieve me of all responsibility. My day was fine, I tried to say, but the words didn't come, just the dry *click* of my jaw opening and closing. His fingers traveled along my side and settled in the hollow of my hip.

I knew he wanted me to make it happen. I had to start, for some reason. It was my job. But I couldn't.

"What went on tonight?" I insisted.

"Nothing special."

You keep expanding love to take in more things, hoping it will become this cure-all, this guarantee of happiness. But then it gets so diluted, so thinned, like a watered-down drink.

"You smell nice," he yawned.

"It's your cologne."

"No. Something else."

"Meat," I said. "Beef tenderloin."

"Mmm."

His body gave a last shake. He slept. He never got up, even in the beginning, when she woke every two hours. Now it was down to once a night, and even that was rare. I was the only one who didn't sleep. My dreams leaked into my days, and my daily concerns transformed themselves into nightmares. I waited another minute, then worked myself free. There was still enough room to be alone, even with him taking up three-quarters of the bed. I lay there and tried not to cry.

· · ·

"I see we have some new people here, which is great. So I think we should go around and introduce ourselves. I'm Janice and this is Louise. Louise was ten pounds eleven ounces at birth."

"Wow," we all said, a chorus.

A few days later, I went to a meeting of the Parallel Play Group. It was at Osbourne's, a coffee shop on Seventh that had a wicker basket of toys kids could play with. There were only eight or nine of us, but with all our stuff we pretty much took over the place. I got a muffin and a cup of coffee and let Ann loose over the red tile floor.

"I'm Alison and this is Dominic. Dominic is named after his father, aren't you, Dominic?"

"Hi, Dominic!"

I didn't know why I had come. For company, maybe. Despite all my bitching, I needed to be with people like me. I was lonely.

But of course the rest of these mothers weren't like me at all. They had this confidence I completely lacked. I got the sense they had already lived their lives, the first part, at least. They'd had deeply meaningful love affairs and jobs, been to Europe and Asia, gone through all the happiness and sadness available to them as single people, and then, just when it was getting tired, when it looked like they might be repeating themselves, they had cashed out at the top of the market, traded in at just the right moment. Now they were entering this new phase. They were eager. That was the difference. Under all the fatigue and drudgery and polite complaining, they were excited.

"Randall just arrived last week. From Guatemala."

"Oh my God!"

"Look at him!"

"He's adorable."

"Hi, Randall!"

There was a pause. All eyes turned to me. I was next. I tried clearing my throat.

"I'm Eve, and this is Ann. She's . . ."

I couldn't think of any cute little fact to add. I felt this absurd need to compete with the kids who had come before. What *was* Ann? What made her special? What set her apart?

"She's a mistake." I tried to imitate their mock-confidential tone. "I mean, an accident."

I gave a nervous laugh. My whole body was turning scarlet. A hot flash. Menopause. Good. I was past childbearing. At last.

"I mean, when I met her father, it was for an *injury*. I had no idea that—"

"Don't I see you in the park?" Janice asked.

"Yes," I answered, as if it was an amazing coincidence.

She was being nice, trying to rescue me, but still it was the kind of exchange I hated, a mindless acknowledgment, assuring each other of our mutual existence.

"She's beautiful."

"Thanks."

"Hi, Ann!" everyone chanted.

I looked down. She was oblivious, banging a plastic xylophone against the wall, her serious, intense face—a miniature version of my own, everyone said, although I couldn't see it—framed by dark hair. She never used a toy the way it was supposed to be played with, which I liked, that rebel quality, most of the time.

"Ann," I chirped, "they're saying hello."

"This is Jeremy," another woman began, uncertain, not sure if our contribution to the morning's entertainment was over. "He's almost six months."

After the initial introductions, none of us mentioned our husbands. We were past the whole concept. Husbands had served their purpose. None of us talked about work, either. Nobody said, "What do you do?" We barely even referred to the weather except for it how it affected taking care of babies. True, there was only so much conversation you could squeeze from which kind of wipes came out of the box better, although, to my horror, I found I had strong opinions on the subject.

"Oh, nothing's worse than scraping your fingers over the top of that block and not finding the folded strip you're supposed to grab for getting a single wipe. You know what I mean? Because meanwhile you're holding down this struggling creature, like a rodeo rider trying to hog-tie a calf, so you end up gouging a hole deep into the 'Lanolin-Treated Wipeaze,' and then you have to live with shreds of stinky wet paper for the next five or six changes. Now, of course there is that hi-tech alternative of the little whale-shaped plastic cylinder that has a blow hole on top where wipes pop up individually. You've seen that, right? But have you ever read the label? It only holds half as many! So it's much more expensive."

I looked around.

"Much more expensive *per wipe*."

There was a silence.

"Does anyone want more coffee?" someone asked.

"Think I've had enough," I mumbled, resolving not to say another word.

I tried not to think about having met Mark in the playground, which meant I thought exclusively about it, getting madder and madder at the way he had looked at me, at the things he had said. Because his whole attitude, the time we'd been together, was one of exaggerated indifference. Come if you want, he seemed to be saying, whenever I used to call, as if it was a favor, allowing me over to his place. But when I did come, he was completely available to me in a way no other man had ever been. What we had was private and all-consuming. But only when he was right in front of me. Each time I left the loft, panic was waiting at the foot of the stairs. I had such good times with him and such bad times without him. And the bad times seemed necessary, part of the experience. There was nothing stable or nourishing about it. He meshed with my life on such a deep level. I needed more of him. More than I could ever have. He knew that. He had to know that. And now for him to show up this way and act as if—

"I really like your shirt," one of them, I think it was Alison, said.

"Thanks."

"Where'd you get it?"

"Third Street."

She had a big bruiser of a boy who was already making little fists and punching her leg.

"Now, Dominic," she said. "Third Street?"

"Oh, it's not a store. I get stuff."

She nodded, the nod that means, You just tried to make sense but failed completely.

"I find things. See, I made this vow, when I had her."

Ann kept reaching for another kid's faucet-of-snot nose, outraged, like it was a toy of hers he had stolen. He began to cry. I broke them up, trying not to notice the green-yellow glue pouring out of each nostril and collecting on his upper lip.

"A vow?"

She was still there. Alison. I had forgotten all about her.

"About clothes." I had Ann in my lap now. "I swore I wouldn't buy anything for myself, after she was born. People leave so much out, in this neighborhood. They just drape it over their fence or fold it up on the top step of their stoop."

"So you—?"

"I guess it's like dumpster diving. Not that I go through garbage cans. Not yet, at least. All I buy for myself are socks and underwear."

"You must save a lot of money that way."

"It's not about money. It's about getting past the illusion of free will. You think you're dressing yourself when you buy clothes, that you're making a choice, saying, This is me. But really you're not, because all your so-called choices have been chosen for you." My voice was too loud. I could feel it forcing its way through me, stumbling on a thought I truly believed. I tried not to shout. "So I figured if I just wore what was out there, other people's rejected or used-up fantasies—about who they were, what they wanted to come across as—and *took those on,* well, maybe that would give me a kind of reverse freedom."

She shot a quick glance off to the side, maybe to see if anyone else had heard and was calling for an ambulance.

"Anyway," I finished, "I thought I would just wear what I found. And I ended up with a lot of good stuff that way. Although now that it's winter, I guess I won't be getting any more things for a while."

I laughed, as if that was the punch line to a really funny joke.

It's parallel play for us, I realized. We're the ones who are alone, oblivious, unable to recognize a fellow creature sitting six inches away. It was hopeless. I couldn't hit that note of quiet, boring conversation. I didn't fit in. What did I expect, that motherhood would give me a free pass into the normal world? I was still a freak, just a freak with a child, now. That was the only difference.

"Well, it's a nice shirt," she said, bringing the conversation back to where it had begun.

"Thanks."

It ended badly, with Ann taking a dump that blasted through all three layers of her outfit. After changing her, I didn't sit back down, didn't say goodbye, just continued on out. We had to be going anyway. She was due for her checkup.

. . .

I thought one of the advantages of marrying Harvey would be free medical care, but he refused to even look at her. They had been warned about that. Either you saw what you wanted to see or were so paranoid you saw what you were afraid of seeing. Instead, he made me go to his friend Mindy, who'd hooked on with a really fancy pediatric practice in Brooklyn Heights. She was this tightly wound woman who wore real outfits, all planned, down to matching shoes and jewelry. Even stockings. I could see them, under her white coat. She always gave me the same look, perpetual surprise at whom Harvey had ended up with.

"How long has she had this?"

"Had what?"

"This."

She pointed to one of Ann's tiny fingers.

"What? It's a knuckle."

"That's the knuckle. Above it."

It was just a bump.

"I don't know."

Here I was, the mother, and this woman who'd examined her for all of fifteen minutes had already seen something I missed. She sighed and shook her head as if it was my fault, then frowned at the finger under a light. Even Harvey admitted

Mindy could be rude, sometimes. "But she's an excellent doctor," he said. "Well, she'd *have* to be," I'd answered.

"You know, she sucks that finger a lot. Maybe it's just a teething bump."

"A teething bump?"

"Yes."

Everyone else seemed to know these fake medical childhood-development terms, so why shouldn't I make one up? Of course using it on a real doctor probably wasn't too brilliant.

"So what is it?" I asked.

"A cyst."

"Is that serious?"

She ignored me, just opened the folder that had Ann's charts in it and made a little note there.

"Let's talk about you, Eve."

Let's not, I thought, starting to get Ann dressed, which was hard enough without an audience. The way she waggled her foot made it impossible to get it through a pant leg. Meanwhile Mindy just sat, watching.

"How's it going?"

"Great."

"Getting any sleep yet?"

"Some."

"Harvey says she pretty much sleeps through the night now."

"Yeah, well I have things on my mind."

"You look good."

"Thanks."

I couldn't figure out if this was her clumsy attempt at socializing or part of the checkup, making sure I wasn't going to lose it and harm my child the minute we hit the street. Ann's toes were stuck in five different directions. I tried burrowing my hand in from the other side. I could feel Mindy judging me.

"What kind of things do you have on your mind that keep you from sleeping?"

"Oh, nothing in particular," I went on in a chatty tone, pretending to be absorbed in what I was doing, which I was, actually, gathering the toes, making sure they didn't bend back and snap off, guiding the little foot through.

"Like what?"

"There!" I stood back, very pleased; the shirt would be easier. "I told you: nothing, really. Why? What did Harvey say?"

"He didn't tell me anything specific. It's more what he implied."

"Which is . . . ?"

"Just that you're stressed out. Have you thought about seeing anyone?"

"You mean like a doctor?"

She nodded.

"I'm seeing you now. And when I get home tonight I'll see Harvey. I don't know, maybe you could say I'm seeing too many doctors. Maybe that's my problem."

I didn't like Mindy, but I admired her. I would have liked to *be* her, in another life. But since I wasn't, she made me say things, bad things. She brought out the worst in me.

"There are therapists," she began, "who specialize in post-partum—"

"There's nothing wrong with me. I'm doing fine."

"You might be depressed."

"If I am depressed, I'm depressed for a reason, which makes it OK."

"There are also medications you can take—"

"That would make me happy even though I don't have a reason to be happy? See, *that*, to me, would be crazy."

"You have plenty of reasons to be happy, don't you, Eve?"

I sighed. Mindy had a job, a career; she had taken control of her life in exactly the way I hadn't. I had just let things happen. And yet I sensed she was just as frustrated as I was, that she even envied me while I was busy envying her. Maybe we did have something to talk about, I didn't know, but I wasn't going to break down and have a heart-to-heart cryfest with her. That would violate some core privacy I had to defend.

I got Ann into her socks and shoes.

"Look, I'm just a pediatrician."

A childless pediatrician, I corrected silently. At least I thought it was silently. I frowned, listening for an echo.

"But you've got to understand that this is not an uncommon occurrence in new mothers."

"I appreciate your concern."

"Without treatment, it can lead to a very serious mental condition. Studies show that—"

"When did you talk to Harvey, anyway?"

"We ran into each other."

I concentrated very hard on the laces.

Someone knocked at the door. It was such a small room she had to brush past me, stepping out to consult with another doctor, one of her bosses. I got Ann's jacket on. I was afraid she was getting reprimanded for taking too long with us. She's just trying to help, I thought. Why do I always want to bite her head off?

When she came back in, our little moment was over.

"So I've been wondering." I acted as if the last part of the conversation hadn't happened, in case I'd been rude. "Should I be doing something?"

"For what?"

"The holidays."

"You mean Hanukkah?"

"I guess. I mean, Harvey hasn't brought it up or anything, but . . ."

"Maybe he doesn't want to make you uncomfortable."

"Why would doing something for Hanukkah make me uncomfortable?"

She started leading us down the hall.

"You have some kind of background in that area, don't you?"

"I was raised in a religious community."

"Right."

"But I don't believe anymore."

"Neither do I, I guess."

She made one last note on a form and handed it to the nurse behind the desk.

"But you're still doing something, aren't you?"

Her hair was pulled back. It made her face smooth, birdlike. She brushed an imaginary strand away from her eyes.

"Yes, as a matter of fact I am, but I doubt Harvey expects to. I don't remember him being particularly observant."

"Yeah. He didn't even observe he was marrying a lunatic. You know what I mean?"

I was going to nudge her, to show I was joking, to show I could tell what she really thought of me, but decided maybe that was going too far.

She gave a brief, pained smile. "Call, if you change your mind."

"About what?"

"What we talked about. I know the names of some excellent people."

• • •

Ann was in the Snugli. I'd sworn I would never wear one. It was the ultimate fashion blunder. I remembered thinking, You spend all that time trying to expel the little parasite from your body, then strap it right back on to your belly again and go around looking sixteen months pregnant? No, thank you. But it turned out to be essential for getting through the folding doors and up the steep steps of city buses. I rested my lips against the top of her head. There was a soft spot I was searching for— Harvey had showed it to me—where the panels of her skull slid together and left a little hole on top. Otherwise she couldn't have made it through the birth canal. It was my favorite area to nuzzle. But the bones were fusing together. It was harder and harder to find.

I had lied to Mindy. I still believed, just not *in* anything. Everyone said they weren't religious but still went through the motions; that's what I didn't understand. Religion *is* the motion, I felt like saying. The motions are the outward signs of who you are. But not for them, I guess. For them it was just social. For me, the world was still a crystalline place, even though the crystal itself had gone. That's what made it come into such incredible focus sometimes, like now, viewed from a bus, removed by height and distance. You could dip into people, imagine for whole seconds at a time being one with them, then slowly pull away, keeping a little of what you had experienced.

A rider pushed the strip of rubberized tape and the NEXT

STOP sign went on with a *ding!* The bus lurched. I came out of my trance, my lips still searching over the hard curve, tasting, feeling for a way past Ann's wispy hair into her brain, wanting to channel my feelings directly, bypass words, kissing her at each bump.

Chapter Three

Mornings started later and later. When the sun did come, all it showed was a white salty crust on everything, as if the last drops of life had been sucked out overnight, a life you didn't realize objects like sidewalks and cars even had until it went away. The tree outside our window was bare. Close up, its sharp branches trembled and jerked, needles on a machine, recording some invisible event.

It's 10 A.M., I reminded myself, watching my shadowy reflection. You're taking care of your baby. This is the most normal situation in the world. You're the most normal person in the world. You think you're weird but really you're not. That's what you can't accept: how ordinary both you and your situation are.

I missed working, hunching over the sewing machine and losing myself for hours at a time, that vaguely sick feeling that came from staying up all night, until the tailor's dummy began to breathe, until I finally figured out how something worked, got inside the designer's head. It was practice, an apprenticeship, but for what? Not the life I was leading now.

The phone rang.

"What are you doing today?"

"Oh." I looked down. I hadn't gotten dressed yet. "Nothing. I mean, I have no plan or anything. How did you get this number?"

"You told me his name."

"I did?"

"Harvey Gabriel, M.D."

"Because I'm not in the book."

"I know."

It was Mark.

Neither are you, I wanted to say. In the book. I checked.

"So I thought maybe we could go to Coney Island. The three of us."

"Are you kidding?"

"You always said you wanted to."

"Have you looked outside? It's freezing."

"That means no one else will be there. We'll have the whole place to ourselves."

"Don't you have some kind of contracting job to do?"

"Pick you up in twenty minutes."

I hung up but didn't let go of the phone. It was typical Mark. He never thought about how anything might seem. Thought was supplied by the people around him. He just focused on staying in touch with his desires. Not that he desired me. It wasn't about me at all. I mean, yes, it was true, I had once talked about going to Coney Island. But the point was, he felt like calling so he did. He was sentimental or guilty or, more likely, bored. So why shouldn't I take advantage, especially since the alternative was shivering in a playground? He was using me and offering that I use him back. That was the only kind of relationship he understood.

"We're going for a ride," I told Ann, beginning to sketch out exactly what I'd need to bring. It was like planning for a military expedition. "A man is going to take us someplace. It's going to be fun."

There you go, I warned. Laying the foundation for a lifetime of disappointment.

"Well, he's fun."

That was true. Mark was fun, even if time with him, in the long run, wasn't.

I got us ready, still in a daze, concentrating just on what was right in front of me, the preparations. At the last minute, I decided to tell Harvey, in case we were gone longer than I thought. I dialed the hospital. He wasn't available, of course.

"Could you tell him—?"

The desk nurse was talking to someone else while she waited to write down what I said. There was all this activity in the background, a whole world, operating at a different speed, with different priorities.

"Yes?"

"Never mind. I'll call back later."

I dug out some old jeans from the bottom of a drawer. Miraculously, they fit. Just the idea of going somewhere made me feel thinner, more energetic. In the mirror, I saw the opposite of usual: I looked older than I felt, but in a good way, more mature and wise and shrewd. A woman, whatever that was. And nothing can happen, I reminded myself, because I have Ann. She was this guarantee I could visit the past and not get stuck there.

"So you have a purpose," I explained, cramming her into a sweater. "Isn't this exciting? You'll actually be performing a function."

We waited upstairs until his pickup truck appeared. Outside, it was even colder than I had imagined.

"Shouldn't you have a child seat?" he frowned.

"Where would we put it?"

The cab only had a trough in back with two fold-down benches on either side, nothing you could attach it to.

"I thought there was some kind of law."

"Don't worry. We'll be fine. How do you even know about that?"

"Know about what?"

"Child seats and stuff?"

"I don't want to get stopped."

I hugged her to my lap and strapped the one belt over both of us.

"Let's *go*."

He took off and, I swear, I felt this husk, the dried-out nutcase of my sad self, get left behind. I could see her, in the passenger-side mirror, standing in front of our building, waving goodbye.

·   ·   ·

"She was looking for space; I was having trouble with the rent."

"So she started out being your sublettor?"

"No. We were already together by then."

"But she was *paying* you?"

"It's not like that, Eve. It just evolved from knowing each other to a monetary situation to this space-sharing, and then finally . . ."

"You got married."

He shrugged, not necessarily agreeing, listening to someone else's version, not his own.

"It's more like we were just acknowledging what was already there."

The morning light, or maybe just seeing him for the second time, made him look older than that day at the playground. But his face, even though it was beginning to show small signs of wear and tear, still hadn't changed from within. Some people arrive at a stage in life and stay, let nature do its worst. He was twenty-four and always would be. That's where his features had decided to make their stand.

"How come you moved?"

"Io wanted to. She said we should buy. She has money, a little."

Ann was in a constant state of reaching, for the evergreen tree–shaped air freshener card, the loose change in the cup holder, for the outside world: houses now instead of brownstones, some with shrubs, and then suddenly a high-rise project surrounded by a barbed-wire parking lot. I felt her body, still so much my own, straining, grabbing. . . .

"So are you going to have kids?" I asked, keeping up this relentless prying, afraid to talk about us.

"I don't know. Should we?"

"If you want."

"What's it like?"

"Great," I replied automatically. I was so conditioned. And of course it was great, in the sense of huge, like the Great Fire of . . . whenever.

My mind drifted off. He stopped the truck.

"This is it? This is Coney Island?"

"We have to walk from here."

"But we didn't cross anything."

"Like what?"

"Like a river. Or a canal."

"It's just called Coney Island. I don't think it really is."

"I know it's just *called* Coney Island, but still I thought there'd be some kind of border. Or at least a sign."

"I'm surprised you've never been, being such an explorer and all."

I didn't want to say this was the one place I'd made sure to never go, because I was afraid of running into him.

He got the stroller out of the back and set it up. It was strange to be a couple again, even in the playacting sense. We crossed a road and went up a ramp, onto the boardwalk. The wind hit us full in the face. Mark was from Wisconsin. I was from Iowa. That was one of our points in common, coming all the way from the Midwest, reaching the end, the ultimate end. It was something I'd always pictured us doing together. And we had finally made it, except it was a joke. We weren't together, and the child wasn't ours—wasn't his, at least. It was like we had rented her for the occasion.

"There's the Ferris wheel," he said. "And the roller coaster. Of course they're closed now."

I had to walk fast to keep up with his long strides. The wind was purifying. It blew away unnecessary thoughts. We shouted over it, so our words were stripped down too. Even the one tear in each eye was a drop of distilled sadness, your heart realizing it couldn't afford to weep.

"Wait, where is that?" I asked, squinting across the ocean. There was land on the other side. It was impossible. Land beyond land. A thin strip of buildings.

He stopped. The wind lifted his hair. He had an earring I didn't remember.

"Is she going to be all right?"

"Who?"

"Her."

"How should I know?"

"You're her mother."

I bent down and looked. Ann had gone into a shrunken old-ladyish hibernation, only her eyes peering out. I should have brought one of those heavy-duty plastic covers, but then it always looked like you were suffocating your child, not that freezing her was any better.

"There's a pier too. People fish off it in the summer. It's nice."

He looked around helplessly. Everything he wanted to show me was gone, closed for the season.

"But where *is* that?" I insisted.

I had thought there would be nothing but emptiness, an edge you could fall over the side of, like when the earth was flat. But instead there were buildings and trees, more ordinary life, this insistent presence, ruining the view.

He gave up pointing out tourist attractions and stared with me, really applying his mind to the problem.

"Japan, maybe?"

I sighed. It wasn't the majestic vision I had been expecting. The city never really ended, just curved in on itself.

We walked, leaning forward into the wind. He tried holding my hand. I coughed and knelt to tie my shoe. That put me at eye level with Ann, who was staring at wave after wave. It didn't seem as cold down here, in childhood. She was content—or in a coma. I passed my fingers in front of her. She didn't blink.

"Maybe we should get her inside," Mark said. "I know a place. If it's open."

I didn't want to leave, though there was really nothing to see.

"You're probably right," I admitted.

He turned the stroller.

Men, I had noticed, were really into driving baby strollers. They made tight turns, did S's around obstacles, like it was a bicycle or their first car. I half expected him to pop a wheelie as I followed, not trying to keep up this time, lingering far enough behind to imagine what it would be like to go past that last strip of houses, to reach the pounding surf on the other side. My toes scrunched up, gripping imaginary sand.

We ate at an ancient hot-dog place that was trying to be fast food but somehow screwed up and tasted good instead. The hot dogs were more like sausages and the French fries were cut so thick they reminded you of potatoes. Even the cardboard trays the cups of soda came in were gray and solid. You could actually make out wood chunks in the process of becoming pulp.

"You ever go home?" I asked Mark.

"Sure. A couple of times. Can I do this?"

He was trying to feed her a French fry.

"When did you start liking kids so much?"

"I always liked kids." He was searching her face, as if it held some secret. "Why? Are you thinking of going back to that weird place where you grew up?"

"It wasn't weird, just different. Did you ever think about having kids with me?"

He shrugged.

"I'll take that for a no."

"You haven't changed."

"Don't be silly. I've done nothing but change."

"Not really."

There was a silence. We were awkward, wondering what we

were doing, having trouble looking at each other, which was why we both focused on Ann. Maybe that's what children are for, I thought. Maybe they're sponges, to soak up excess emotion.

"So honestly," he asked, "what's it like?"

"Parenthood? I don't know. Once, I heard a guy say, 'I have muscles in places where other people don't even have places.' It's kind of like that. You find yourself getting strong in areas you didn't even know existed before."

He was waiting for her to eject a wad of half-chewed potato. He had a quiet way of listening without responding, as if he was taking in what you said on a deeper nonverbal level, really getting it. Although at other times, I remembered, when I was mad at him to start with, he had acted the exact same way and just seemed dumb. All he did now was very delicately put one French fry in his mouth and slowly bite down, showing her how.

"Who'd you come here with?" I asked. "Before, I mean."

"No one."

He was still looking at Ann.

"You came here by yourself?"

"A couple of times."

"That's not like you."

. . . because even though he acted very aloof and self-sufficient, Mark hated to be alone.

"After you left, I'd just come here and hang out."

"Why?"

"You talked so much about this place. I thought I might see you."

"After I left?" I echoed stupidly. "Wait a minute, I never left. You're the one who—"

"Let's not talk about it."

To make sure I wouldn't say any more, he reached out and ran his fingers through my hair. They caught against all the snarls and tangles, giving my head a sharp tug.

   •   •   •

On the way home, I picked a fight with him. I could feel it coming. We had walked more. He played with Ann, which I appreciated but also found irritating. I saw her responding, eyes shining, waving her arms, all in this crude imitation of how I had once been, falling for his charm. Not that there's anything wrong with charm, I thought, watching. Immediately, I corrected myself—yes, there was something wrong with charm. I just couldn't remember what—as he mesmerized her, hiding his face with his hands, pretending to disappear and then popping up just when she didn't expect it.

"Peek-a-boo!"

She stared at this new planet that had loomed into view, blocking out everything else in her sky.

Back in the truck, he looked around, decided it was safe, and pulled out a half-smoked joint. That's when I got mad, or what I chose to get mad about, although I didn't say anything, just rotated my lap so she couldn't see.

Ann sensed I was taking her away from him and strained to get back. She was hooked.

"You want me to open a window?"

"No."

He did anyway, a crack, blowing the smoke out each time and then closing it up. We were in that part of Brooklyn where Orthodox Jews lived. Men, all in black, with hats made of dark waterproof-looking fur, walked alongside women who had four, five, even six children. The older girls helped out with the younger ones. The progression was so gradual you couldn't see, driving past, where daughter ended and mother began.

"Io's worse than you are, about this."

He was holding his breath.

"Good."

"She won't even let me do it in the loft unless we're having a party or something. I have to go up on the roof."

"Why did you call?" I demanded. "I mean, what did you expect to happen today?"

"I thought it would be fun to get together."

Ann was a gyroscope, veering back to the source of her pleasure, getting agitated when I tried redirecting her gaze.

"Sure you don't want any?"

"No. Thank you. It's just weird to me that you're still doing this."

"Getting high?"

"Playing with people's minds."

"I'm not—"

"It's the perfect situation for you, isn't it? I'm home alone with a kid, and you can just call me up and be this white knight on his pickup truck who takes me off for a few hours of escape from my dull depressing life and then drops me off right back where I started from, while you—"

"I wanted to see you."

"And, no, you shouldn't still be smoking pot."

I turned to him now, in Full Nag Mode. Ann, who probably thought he'd gone away, started making awful wanting noises, these asthmatic grunts.

"OK."

He flicked the joint out the window.

"That's not what I meant. You shouldn't be doing any of this, Mark. You should be moving on to something new."

"Like what?"

"I don't know. That's for you to decide."

He gripped the wheel very carefully with both hands, concentrating on his driving.

"So your life is dull and depressing?"

"No."

"That's what you said."

"I did not! I said that's what you were making it out to be, with this little pity expedition."

"So you're happy."

"Of course I'm happy."

I held Ann close.

You just had to reacquaint yourself with certain basic emotions. Redefine them. This might not look or feel or sound like happiness, I told myself, not to the uninitiated, but in fact—I stuck my chin out—this was happiness now, so much more complex and rich a sensation than happiness used to be. I couldn't even remember a single instance of being happy in my old life. Not really.

"I'm glad," he said.

What are you doing? I suddenly asked myself. Why are you sliding back into all these shopworn fantasies about a guy there is absolutely zero chance of your ever sleeping with again?

We pulled up in front of the apartment building. The anger I thought I was getting out of my system swirled around me, a backwash of guilt, as he helped us down, got the stroller out too, and the diaper bag.

"That's all right," I said, standing there, helpless. "You don't have to do that."

"Hey, we finally went to Coney Island."

"Yeah. It was great."

He smiled. We had relived our whole relationship, from getting together to being a couple to breaking up, all in the space of a few hours, just running our emotions over it, as if this was some kind of healing exercise. And now it was over. Really over.

"So," he said.

"Well, thanks." I hurried to gather all the equipment, to fill my hands even more, not knowing how we would say goodbye. "Thanks for everything."

"Want me to help you get upstairs?"

"No! I mean, really, it's fine. You've done enough. I had a great time."

I didn't watch him go. I let Ann do that, holding her over my shoulder while I opened the door to the building so she could stare behind. But she was tired. It had been a long day. I could feel her body going limp. She didn't know who he was, anymore.

* * *

"It's the Rockaways." Harvey was in the bathtub. I was in the living room. "Breezy Point, Belle Harbor, Far Rockaway. The Atlantic Ocean's on the other side."

"You've been there?"

"Sure."

Of course he's been there, I thought. He'd been everywhere, without having moved a muscle.

"Who is this guy anyway?"

"An old friend."

"And he just called, out of the blue?"

"I think he wanted to see what it was like. Having children."

I said it as one of those automatic white lies and then wondered if that really was the reason Mark had come around. Maybe he thought he could practice on Ann, see what it felt like to be a dad, just as, before, maybe he had been practicing on me, seeing what it would be like to be a husband.

"So what did you tell him?"

"That it was great."

"Do you want to have them over for dinner some night?"

"Who?"

"That friend of yours and his wife."

"Oh, no."

"Why not?"

"He's not really a friend."

A few minutes later he came into the room, naked. My eyes went to the parts of him I particularly liked, his hands, very big and caring, his shaggy eyebrows. He sat down next to me and I laid my head on his chest, a rough blanket, thick and warm, the kind you could wrap yourself up in and survive any winter night. I missed Harvey. Even with him right here, I missed him. If a totally different man had come out of the bathroom, I wondered, how long would it take me to notice? And when I did, would I act any differently?

"So what are you going to do?" he asked.

"I don't know."

Tomorrow was my big day. He had just found out he wasn't working, for once. He wanted me to go off by myself and let him take care of Ann. I said we should spend it together, a family day, but he had this picture of me wandering around, carefree, doing all the things I wasn't able to do normally.

"Maybe get a haircut."

"That sounds good."

I tried to think of something else. I didn't want him to be angry that I couldn't come up with more solo activities.

"What about you? What would you do, if you had a day to yourself?"

He shook his head.

"It's different for me. There hasn't been such a break."

"Why?"

"It's not like I had alternate lives I could have led."

"What do you mean?"

"Well, when you were talking about that guy . . ."

"Mark?"

"It made me think you must have been wondering what it would be like if you ended up with him instead of me."

"That's so completely wrong. The man I'm with isn't the sole determining factor of what kind of life I'm going to live."

"I never said it was."

"You're just jealous."

"Of course."

His eyes got that faraway look. He could go away in the middle of a conversation, pull a vanishing act. You had to shake him, reconnect him to his surroundings.

"I want to get a job," I announced.

His hand, which had fit itself over the top of my skull and was massaging behind my ears, stopped for a moment, then went on.

"That's great."

"No, it's not." I tried rolling over, away from him. Except he was everywhere. I was staring between his legs. "Because what it would cost to put her in day care is probably more than I could make while she was gone."

"You could always go back to what you did before."

"Make knockoffs? And take care of her at the same time?"

The male body was still a mystery to me. You'd think by now that would be the *last* thing it contained, mystery, but I couldn't get used to how external it was. Up close, I watched him expand, the little accordion folds, wrinkles, but not the wrinkles of age. Pleats.

"People say how much things have changed," I said, "with the wife working and the husband helping, but I don't see it happening. If the wife works, she still ends up doing the parenting and the housework too. Either that or she gives up the kid completely, and then what was the point of having one in the first place?"

It sounded like something from a magazine article, but I didn't care. I was dimly aware of what was really going on. I was using Mark, the idea of Mark, to reignite my feelings for Harvey. And maybe Harvey's feelings for me. It was wrong, but something about it being wrong made it very deeply right. For both of us. His hands had come alive.

So this is marriage, I thought. When you actually know how things work. What did it say about me, that I was being so cold-blooded? Well, somebody had to be. Romance was not just going to spring up around us like some perfumed flower. The simple truth was, I was tired of not-making-love. We'd been not-doing-it, actively not-having-sex, every night. It wasn't so much that I wanted to, anymore, as that I wanted to get it over with. The tension had worn me out, made me desperate and crazy and no longer myself.

He was trying to get me to go back to the bedroom with him. There were no curtains in the living room. I wanted to stay, though. I liked the idea of people watching us, of their finding us interesting enough to *want* to watch. He began to lift me and I shook my head.

"Come," he said.

He was hard now, and I was half undressed but for some reason still resisting.

"So you see it's really not so great if I want to get a job. There's no way I can go back. I'm stuck."

"Stuck," he repeated, like that was a good thing. Something to be desired.

He tried to carry me.

I was mad at him. I'd been talking without really listening to what I said, just playing a part, and then, cumulatively, it all came to me: I was furious at his physical presence in my life, at what he'd gotten me into. I was furious specifically at his arm, scooping under my shoulders. I nestled my chin into that familiar husbandy smell and bit down once, hard.

"Jesus!"

He almost dropped me. His knee came up to prop my back. He twisted his shoulder to get a better look. I hadn't even broken the skin.

"Bitch," he added wonderingly.

"Prove it," I said.

His eyes returned to mine and finally we were on familiar ground. I don't know how we had gotten there, by some weird roundabout route, a hidden passageway full of rats and spiders, but we were both back to a place we remembered. A power flowed through our limbs. Our thoughts combined and thickened.

Ann made a gurgling sound.

"What was that?" he frowned.

"Nothing. You're right. Let's go to the bedroom."

"Did she laugh?"

Neither of us had remembered her. She was asleep in the swing, or had been. God knows how long she'd been up, taking in a scene that was probably right out of some textbook on What Causes Mental Disorders.

"I think she laughed," he said.

"She did not laugh."

I could taste him. There was a neat crescent of toothmarks on his forearm. I was already, in my mind, deeply involved in what was to follow.

"Did you laugh, sweetheart?"

He dumped me on the futon, went away, and came back wearing pants.

"Did Annabelle laugh?" he asked, her not me, carefully extracting her from the swing seat.

"Well, even if she did," I argued, trying to replay the sound in my head, "think about what she was seeing when she did it."

"Still, it's her first time."

"I think she was just choking on something." I didn't feel a shred of maternal instinct. The opposite, whatever that would be. Normal, rational thinking? Rediscovering your intelligence? "Let's see if she'll go down. It's almost bedtime anyway. Maybe we can still—"

"I'm going to call my mother. It's not too late."

"Your mother? Why?"

"To tell her. It's a big deal, Eve. She laughed!" He looked at me. "Maybe you should get dressed."

My pants were down around my ankles. I left them that way, trudging past the still-steamy bathroom. It was funny. I tried imagining what she'd seen, peering through her small, clear eyes. I mean, there was something funny about what we'd been doing. You had to admit. Not the kind of funny that made you laugh, though.

. . .

But Marjorie did, when I told her. She laughed so hard she had to put down her cup and saucer so she wouldn't spill.

"You're fine," she finally said. "Look, all mothers go through this. You're supposed to be the Virgin Mary and you're not. Big deal."

"I thought having a child was supposed to reprioritize my life."

She started to laugh again, then saw I was serious.

"The real question you should be asking yourself is: What am I doing here?"

"I wanted to talk."

"Well, I'm flattered, but if I had a whole day off I'm not sure this is where I'd choose to spend it."

We were at her house. What had been her house. She and Sherman were having money troubles since the split and had decided to sell. Stuff was in boxes—or black plastic garbage bags, if it was meant to be thrown away. There were Post-its everywhere because she tried not to be around when he came. Some said, *Yours*. Others, with this accusation you could almost hear, just in the way she'd written the word twice, once on top of the other, said, **Yours**.

"This is not going to happen to you, Eve."

She'd been watching me take it in. Ian and Alex were climbing over piles of crumpled-up newspaper, grabbing fistfuls of packing peanuts, survivor children after a war, playing in rubble.

"Why not?"

"Well, for one thing, Harvey very clearly adores you."

She had out the fine china. White with gold rims. I was terri-fied of breaking something. Unasked questions loomed: Because Harvey adores me? So it's up to him if we stay together or not? I don't have any say in the matter? Didn't Sherman adore *you*, once upon a time? He must have. So what happened? Why couldn't the same thing happen to me too? I tried thinking of various ways to steer the conversation to some safe neutral topic.

"Oh, before I forget." She gave me the keys. "Every two or three days is fine. The watering can's on the counter. There's cat food in the closet. Don't bother to change the litter."

"You have a cat? I didn't know that."

"He's shy."

"Where is he?"

"Under the bed. He never comes out for strangers."

"How come?"

"He was traumatized as a kitten, they think. We got him from an animal rescue shelter."

"What's his name?"

She narrowed her eyes.

"Fauntleroy. He's pretty much the forgotten guy around here. Since the twins. You don't want these, do you? It's a setting for twelve."

"The dishes? Aren't you going to take them?"

"I don't know if I should or not. His family paid for almost all of them. They made us register at Tiffany's. It seems wrong, somehow."

Marjorie's life was just as half packed as all the crap it had gathered. She wasn't even sure what she could take, what she was entitled to. None of the Post-its said **Mine**. It was so sad. I couldn't think of a thing to say.

"Personally," she went on, solving the problem of what to talk about, "I would sleep with any UPS man."

"Because of the uniform?"

"That, and because they're both strong and intelligent-seeming. And they come bearing gifts. But I think the real reason is because I read somewhere that their vans have a skylight, a section of plastic in the roof. So we could do it in the truck, with all these boxes around us, on that metal with the special raised pattern. What's it called?"

"Skid-resistant."

"Right. For some reason that appeals to me."

I held up my cup. The porcelain was so thin you could see through to the other side.

"We almost never used them. Just once or twice, on special occasions. I guess this qualifies."

She was quiet for a minute.

"Are you all right, Marjorie?"

"Sure. Why?"

"I don't know."

She seemed out of it, but in a pleasant way. Not as bitter as usual. I looked again at the boys. They were fine, not dirty or neglected. And the house, even in the act of dying, was cleaner than mine had ever been or ever would be. Still, there was an awkwardness I couldn't locate the source of. We weren't connecting.

"Where is she, anyway?"

"Who?"

"Harvey's mother."

"At some assisted-living facility in Florida."

"You like her?"

"She's all right."

"What about you? Why aren't you calling *your* mother when her granddaughter laughs for the first time?"

"She doesn't have a phone."

"Really?"

"No phones in the Bible."

"So write her a letter, instead of—"

She started wrapping her cup in paper, even though she hadn't rinsed it out yet.

"Instead of what?"

"I'm going to get them some applesauce. Does Annie want any? Oh, that's right, she's with him. I forgot."

"Instead of coming around here?"

She sat back down with a jar and fed the twins one spoonful at a time. They stayed on the floor with their mouths open, baby birds poking their beaks out of the nest. She took a bite herself. Then another.

"You never talk about it," she said.

"The Colony? What's to talk about? It's where I grew up."

"It doesn't sound normal, from what little you do say."

"Whose home life was normal? Was yours?"

"At least we had a telephone."

I sighed.

"There's no point in writing my mother a letter. She wouldn't open it. I'm dead to her."

"Don't be ridiculous. How can you even talk that way?"

"I'm dead to her spiritually."

"Does she know you're married?"

"I'm not, in her eyes. My being married to someone like Harvey wouldn't interest her."

"What would?"

"If I found God." I thought about it for a minute. "Or someone like Him."

"Listen, you've got a day off, Eve. Make use of it. Do something. Go shopping, or go somewhere out-of-the-way and scream, or . . . go on a pilgrimage, if that's what you need to do."

"A pilgrimage? Where to?"

"I don't know." She looked around. "But don't waste your time sitting here with me. Besides, I have to pack."

• • •

I went to Manhattan. It wasn't the same, though. It occurred to me that maybe the reason places didn't seem as loaded with meaning as they used to was because I walked over a landscape of time, instead. *Mother*, for example, had meant one thing all my life, and now it meant another, without replacing the first. I found myself ten years old in one thought and forty-five in the next. The only solid thing left, I discovered, was Ann. Without her, I was a prisoner released from leg irons, full of spastic energy that sent me staggering in circles, unsteady, without any sustained purpose, desperate to get locked up again.

"I'm looking for some kind of Jewish gift."

The salesman didn't understand.

"This is Brooks Brothers, ma'am."

Again with the ma'am, I thought. What did I have to do, wear a bikini?

"It's for Hanukkah. I was thinking of a smoking jacket. Do you have those?"

He hesitated, then finally motioned for me to follow.

"This way."

My brilliant plan (it had just come to me, walking past the store) was to give Harvey a present. I would look at a few things, get some ideas, and then make him his own personal knockoff. It would be a love offering, my first piece of work since having Ann. I'd really have to examine the item, though, especially since it was men's clothes, which I'd never tried copying before. But how hard could it be? The main quality of menswear was its incredible dullness. That's why I asked to see the smoking jackets, because they were the only fancy things guys wore that were even the slightest bit sensual.

"But I don't smoke." I could already hear Harvey's puzzled response.

And then I would explain to him how what he wore was the fashion equivalent of our relationship, and if he put on something that looked and felt special then maybe what we did next would look and feel special too, especially if we drugged Ann first with Infant Tylenol and locked her in a closet. Also dropped a nuclear bomb on the state of Florida. It made perfect sense to me, although I did have trouble visualizing anything so seductive actually *on* him, especially when we came to a headless mannequin in a wild paisley jacket with shiny silk lapels.

"And the silk, of course, continues on the inside as a quilted lining."

"Of course."

"Would this be for any particular club? Because we do offer to monogram in a variety of organizational insignias."

"No. It's just for . . . sitting around the menorah."

"I see."

I didn't really know what Hanukkah was. I mean, I knew the

relevant text (II Maccabees 3:6) but had no clue what people did to celebrate. It wasn't a big issue, Harvey being Jewish and me being a former Tertiary Baptist. Unlike Marjorie, when he learned how I'd been raised, he only asked a few questions and didn't pry, which I appreciated. I was so used to people's rude curiosity. "What was it like?" they'd ask. Just like your childhood, I wanted to answer, except more pure, the hard liquor of Faith and Fall, not the warm beer of "growing up." But I found it impossible to even think about the Colony, much less put what had happened to me there into words. Instead, I'd mumble something about Bible Studies and make it sound as boring as possible. That was beginning to change, though. A month ago, he had asked if I wanted a tree.

"What, one of those little ones the Japanese grow?"

"No, not a bonsai," he explained patiently. "A Christmas tree."

"You mean an evergreen? That's not Christian, it's pagan."

"Oh. I didn't know."

"No Christmas trees in the Bible."

"So was there anything special you did around this time of year?"

"Fasting and prayer," I said, with sudden vehemence.

"Fasting and prayer." I could see him translating that into some sane-world equivalent. "Well, you want to do that? Would it make you happy?"

What would make me happy is you, in this smoking jacket, I answered now, fingering one that was crushed red velvet with orange stripes. I liked how hideous they were. Men trying to be pretty. Their dark secret. It tied with two lengths of thick ribbon. I imagined pulling the knot apart with my teeth.

"That's a Sulka."

The salesman pretended to admire my good taste.

"How much is it?"

"Seven-ninety-nine."

Material would be the major expense. Then there was the padding. The shoulders were absurdly square. I really didn't know how to do collars that well, either. Not this kind. It was going to be harder than I thought.

"Can I try it on?"

There was an awkward moment.

I had always worn the item. It was part of my routine when I was ripping something off. Asking was never a problem. I would go into the dressing room and examine myself from all sides. I realized though, in this setting, how the request might seem odd.

"Just to see how it hangs."

"We don't have a changing area for women."

"Well, I'm not going to get naked. I could just slip into it right here."

He put his hand on the empty sleeve, protecting the crushed velvet, and looked me up and down.

"I think not," he said.

* * *

Before, you would have found a way, I scolded myself, back on the street. Before, you didn't mind making a fool of yourself, as long as you were a holy fool.

They weren't afraid of me, anymore. I had gone from being all dangerous potential to becoming one plain disappointing fact. Even without Ann, when I was given a day off and tried making a pilgrimage to my former self, they saw right through me, as if I had the word MOTHER tattooed on my forehead.

Where to go? A coffee shop, that's where I used to hole up when I felt this way. Sit at the counter, have a cup of coffee and a toasted corn muffin, bland, comforting tastes and textures. But now I was so sensitive about my weight, paranoid my whole metabolism had slowed. Just walking, I noticed people refusing to acknowledge my personal space, that thin lubricating boundary between myself and the world. They stepped on my heel or clipped my shoulder as they went by, not even saying, Sorry. I was traveling at a different speed, or maybe not even traveling at all, a rock in a stream. I kept going, adjusting my stride, searching for that lost rhythm, the way I used to connect with the city, the way *in* I used to have that once, not so long ago, I took for granted.

I could go back to all my old apartments. I could revisit every place I used to work. I could walk to Greene Street and, even though he didn't live there anymore, stand under the window of Mark's old loft. I knew how it would feel, though. I knew how everything would feel. Every thought my mind came upon felt used, not a thought at all, really, but a memory. The depressing fact was I couldn't go back to being a single girl in Manhattan, letting chance choose my direction, trusting the lights would guide me toward my goal. She was gone, that Eve, and replaced by nothing, no one, yet.

I gave up and went down into the subway.

I couldn't believe it. All this time I had groaned about being tied to a kid and then, the one day I was given away from her, I couldn't think of anything to do. My main accomplishment so far was confirming how empty my old life had been. That's why the past echoed so harshly in it. Before, there had been nothing to absorb the sadness or the happiness. Now, being a mother, it was the opposite. Every little thing that happened to me stuck. I could feel myself getting bigger and bigger, becoming encased in layers of history and emotion.

It was dark by the time I turned onto Seventh Avenue. People were buying last-minute ingredients for dinner, hurrying home. Footsteps rang out: all this purpose, clacking and clattering around me. I willed myself back into the flow of things, not bumping into strangers anymore. I let the current carry me along, falling in behind a perfect family: husband, wife, child. That's what I wanted to be. They looked so right together. A unit. I studied them, as if I could learn something. How he pushed the stroller. How she walked in step with him.

I thought I felt a snowflake hit my forehead, but couldn't tell; maybe it was just a bead of sweat. I stopped and gazed at a streetlight to see if anything was outlined against it, that first dusting that brings a crowd together. I wanted to be the one to say, "Look, it's snowing!" and have everyone go, "Ah!" But it wasn't. I squinted into the halo of glare. There was nothing. When I started walking again, the perfect family was farther ahead, turning down the same street I was going to take. The man's face became visible as they crossed, and it was Harvey, pushing Ann. My whole body instantly adjusted to the outside temperature, became 10 degrees, a solid square of puckered sidewalk. I could feel people walking over me, their boots and heels hammering my heart. He was saying goodbye to the woman. She was going in a different direction. He gave her a quick hug. She looked up at him. Both their expressions were grave, as if they had been through some super-serious life-altering ordeal together. He kissed her, on the cheek. She walked away.

It was Mindy.

Chapter Four

New Year's Eve never came to Iowa. Once, I snuck out of the old abandoned summer camp where our group had settled and ran into town. At a bar with a TV near the window, I stood outside, panting so hard the glass fogged up, and thought, I made it! But I hadn't. I had forgotten about the time difference. The new year was already old. It had begun an hour ago, in Times Square. Instead, the local station trained its one camera on a big clock. When the second hand finally got to twelve, they played music—I could hear it inside, mixed with drunken cheering—and fingertips you weren't supposed to notice sprinkled confetti in front of the lens, just a pinch, like a condiment.

Harvey was still surprised.

"I can't believe you said yes."

"Why? Do you mind?"

"No. I think it's a good idea. But you've been so against doing anything, going anywhere."

"I thought it might be fun. We don't get out enough."

He shook his head. I knew what he was thinking. Here it was, the end of the "holiday season" and we hadn't done a thing, just counted off the days as if they were an ordeal, something to get through, both of us sensing it was a minefield, the family gatherings, the fake religion, the gift-giving. And then, just at the end, when it looked as if we were past whatever we were so determined to avoid, for me to blow it this way. . . .

"I'm not good on the phone," I lied. "He caught me off guard."

I wanted to take his hand, but he was pushing the stroller.

What I'd seen hadn't sunk in. I tried to explain it away, view it in a positive light. He was having his own harmless flirtation, maybe lamenting a move he'd never made, one of those alternate lives he thought only women could have. That's when I was feeling charitable. The other twenty-three-and-a-half hours of the day I wanted to make an appointment with my friendly family pediatrician and scratch her eyes out. Then I'd pull out of it for whole minutes at a time and realize I was making most of this up. I'd seen nothing, just a hug and a kiss. Not some passionate smoldering embrace. I was deliberately trying to make myself paranoid and miserable. Harvey was the one positive thing in my life. Why was I so determined to destroy that? Why, when Mark called, had I practically jumped at the chance to go to his party?

"So what does he do again?"

"He's a carpen— a contractor."

"And his wife?"

"I've never met her. I think he said she was a dancer."

I could feel my heart racing as we got closer. This was not a good idea. At least he had moved, so going to the new loft wouldn't be some momentous return. Not that it would have been anyway. My time with Mark was a memory that shrank as

I approached it. Set next to what had happened since, it wasn't that big a deal at all. I had just chosen to make it one, in retrospect.

He's a sign of my own maturity, I decided. I see him now for what he is, what he always was: a nice guy, but sad.

I walked faster, strengthened by this new way of looking at things. We were heading downhill, toward the water. By the time we found the building, I felt infinitely superior in every way. Poor Mark. All he could do was break my heart. That's a pretty pitiful skill when you think about it, compared to Dr. Harvey Gabriel, who had put it back together again. You tell me, who's the better choice?

You didn't have a chance to *choose* Mark, a pesky voice reminded. He dumped you, remember?

No. Technically, I made it so he had no other option but to stop calling.

Or pick up the phone when you called. Or answer his buzzer, for a straight forty-five minutes.

That was one time and it was more of a joke, really.

Then how about when you stood under his window an entire night until he had to come down with a sweater and—?

"Pretty funny, him living in a place called Dumbo." I tried drowning out the evil-bitch-twin-sister inside me.

"It stands for Down Under the Manhattan Bridge Overpass."

"I know. But still, why would you want to call your neighborhood that? I mean, is it reserved for people with low IQs?"

Harvey smiled. "You wouldn't know about Dumbo, growing up where you did."

"You mean he was a person?"

"Dumbo was a flying elephant. His ears were so big they could flap like wings."

"You're kidding. How'd they do that? With wires and stuff?"

"It was a cartoon, Eve."

"Oh."

A freight elevator came down, a big rusty box where you could see the exposed brick of the shaft. Harvey locked the stroller wheels as if we might be swung from side to side. Ann gazed from one of us to the other, so trusting.

"So what else don't I know about, besides flying elephants?"

"Is something wrong?" he asked.

"What do you mean?"

"I don't know. Lately, I get the impression something's eating you."

"She is. About six times a day."

"That's not what I meant."

Words crowded into my brain. All the wrong ways of putting it. All the wrong ways of introducing the subject. I love you, was what I really wanted to say. I love you and please don't leave me. But those words, the simplest of all, I had to practice a million times before I could let them out, before I could loose them on the world. Words that used to come so easily, that had never even needed to be said.

The doors opened.

I was wrong about the loft. Even though he had moved, it was exactly the same, perfectly preserved, like one of those displays in a museum that show an ancient landscape, a diorama, with maybe a stuffed animal or two, and some native hunched over a fire or performing a ritualistic dance.

Harvey's stare was fixed on the ceiling.

"They're Gro-Lites," I explained.

I realized I should have prepared him more, that the stuff I had taken so much for granted might seem to him, an outsider, strange.

They were the same lamps as on Greene Street, attached all along the pipes of the sprinkler system. Each was focused on a plant, one of forty or fifty pot plants in big plastic tubs. The leaves broke out into five points that spread like fingers.

"Eve!" Mark was half hidden behind a large bush. He was plucking leaves one by one and dropping them into a shiny metal bowl. "You're early. Hold on a sec, I'm still getting ready. Io!"

He was shirtless.

Oh, this is not a good idea, I thought again. Why hadn't I pictured what it would be like?

My eyes followed the pattern his muscles made from where he did his sit-ups each day. It was the same as what was painted on an airport runway, showing the planes where to go, as they coasted forward and down with their engines practically shut off, their wheels lowered, their lights flashing. . . . A landing strip.

Since I was momentarily tongue-tied, Harvey moved ahead, pushing Ann in. Then I got past the little blip seeing Mark always seemed to produce in me and introduced them. Almost immediately, more guests came, so he moved off without really saying much. That gave us a chance to look around some more. Harvey was grinning.

"What?" I asked.

"Nothing."

A sink, a stove, and some countertops were set up. Otherwise, it was still a construction site. Sawdust and nails had been cleared away for the party. Sections of raw Sheetrock formed a bedroom wall. We stood in the workshop. There was a table saw and all Mark's tools, which I recognized because he spray-painted every handle fluorescent pink, so on a job there would never be any confusing what was his.

"This is great," Harvey said with real enthusiasm, looking around.

"You like it?"

"Yeah, it's so not me."

That softened me a little, sensing he felt trapped, or at least encumbered, by his situation too. It gave me a thrill. I liked having something to fix, a mission. Rescue Harvey, I put on my mental To Do list.

The floor was scorched black in places. It rippled. The grain of the wood had risen to the surface.

"Fire," Mark explained, coming back. "Then water. A long time ago. I took off about sixteen coats of paint. I was going to sand more, but it looked nice this way. Like a map."

Then he saw Ann and just lit up. I'd never met a guy so into kids.

"Can I hold her?"

"Sure."

He bent over. She laughed, gave a short pleased giggle. Of recognition? I looked at Harvey to see if he noticed, but he had walked over to the first row of plants. Mark balanced her with one palm under her belly. She floated, arms waving, staring down at the floor.

"Male/female?" Harvey asked.

"That's right."

"Why alternating?"

"It works better that way. For pollination."

I was torn between disgust at his nipple ring, which I would never have allowed him to get, and sadistically wanting to see what would happen if she grabbed it. She had a strong grip. Sometimes I thought she couldn't tell the difference yet between her mouth and her hands. Touching was like chewing to her. So was staring. So was everything. She was chewing up the world, digesting it, making it hers.

"What are you two talking about?"

"The plants," Harvey said. "They're male and female, alternating."

"Plants have a sex?"

"Of course."

"How did you know that?"

"It's biology. The ones with . . . tassels"—he looked over—"are male?"

Mark nodded.

"And the ones with flowers are female."

"Oh, so it's just what you call them."

"It's science." He rubbed a leaf between his thumb and forefinger.

"Which is just what you *call* things," I insisted, lumping them together for the first time as Men. "Why is it so hot in here, anyway?"

I was trying not to look at the nipple ring. The way it went *into* him and then came out, the other side. It sent this involuntary shiver through me.

"The whole heating system's out of whack. I got to wrap the pipes. The plants like it, though. They're out of control."

They started talking, this conversation about buildings and mortgages and wiring. I was grateful to Harvey. It wasn't his natural thing, but he was definitely making an effort. Mark, meanwhile, was less embarrassing than I'd feared, except for his nakedness, which seemed to grow as he swooped and dipped

Ann with one hand, bending low and brushing her past a plant, sticking his arm way out and rotating her in a half circle, like an ad for some trendy new exercise fad, Small Child Tai Chi.

"What I want to do eventually is make another level. Build loft beds. Increase the floor space down here."

"How many square feet have you got?"

I walked off without their noticing, deeper into the jungle. Music was coming from the other side. Past one last plant, I found an oasis, a corner of space by the windows. Because what he grew, I remembered, could never be visible from the street. Instead there had to be a show of regular living, a stand-up lamp, a braided rug, an armchair. It was like a stage set, an attempt to make a room where there were no walls. A boom box on the floor was playing classical music. A girl with pigtails was reading a book.

"Are you Eve?" she asked, not looking up.

"I'm sorry," I said. "I didn't know anyone else was here."

"I'm almost finished. Can you wait a minute?"

"Sure."

She was probably around my size. It was hard to tell, because she was sitting down. She wore glasses—the small rimless kind, granny glasses—had watery brown hair and a serious face. She wasn't dressed up at all. I mean, even I had made some token attempt to look festive. But it was her shoes I really noticed. They were black and squared-off and had laces, the kind you'd wear if you lost your toes in an accident. I almost said, You *can't* be Iolanthe but just waited until she finished, looked up, and smiled.

"I'm Io," she said, holding out a hand.

I wondered if I had heard wrong, that time in the playground. Not a dancer but . . . a math teacher? Or one of those lawyers who defend people who chain themselves to trees? I hadn't consciously thought about it but just assumed she would have enormous dark eyes, be five-ten, and weigh maybe eighty-seven pounds.

"Where's your husband?"

"Harvey? With Mark."

"I should be out there too."

"It's a beautiful space."

She wrinkled her nose.

"It's still such a mess. Mark had all these great plans when we moved in. But he's been busy running around, doing stuff, instead."

Like going to Coney Island, I thought.

More people were coming now. The elevator doors opened. Voices came through the wall of plants.

"What are you reading?"

"I'm a member of a book group. We get together once a month."

"That's nice."

"It's all women."

Of course, I almost answered.

"Io!" Mark called.

"You should come, if you want. It's fun."

She got up. I was amazed again at how much she was not a dancer. She was sturdy and kind of plain.

"He talks about you all the time."

She said it in a neutral way, not angry, just throwing it out there.

The spot we were standing on must have been the heart of the fire. It was more pitted and full of mounds than the rest. I stumbled, trying to follow her, wanting to answer, He talks about you all the time too, but realized that would sound bad, somehow. Not to mention the fact that it wasn't true.

"So how did you guys meet?" I called ahead.

"He was doing some work for my parents."

They're drug dealers?

I found I was having this totally invisible conversation. Every one of the sentences that came into my head was wrong. Luckily, she didn't seem to mind doing most of the talking.

"They have a townhouse on the East Side. Mark and his crew were redoing the library."

His crew?

"You mean he really is a contractor?" That one got out, but at the last minute I managed to remove the surprise from my voice.

"He's good. Well, you know." She held back a branch for me. It was like we were trekking, except she was taking me off to the side, not back to the party itself. The loft was huge. "And I was living at home."

So you had this half-naked hunky carpenter guy getting a glass of water and sitting down with you in the kitchen, I filled in mentally. And since you were looking for an apartment and he was looking for someone to share the rent with, before you knew it—

"This is going to be my part. When it's done."

It was where all the clothes were now, a storage area, with half-open suitcases, a pile of laundry, some boxes still sealed with tape. Framed pictures and posters leaned against the wall. The only sign of what she did, if you could even call it that, was a yoga mat unrolled on the floor.

"Where do you know him from?" she asked, taking off her shirt.

I guess she had the right, since I had just put the same question to her. Still, it felt weird. Plus her changing right in front of me.

"Oh, it's funny," I said, looking away. "I was taking this course, Fashion Illustration, which was about sketching clothes. But for the first week we were supposed to do life studies, draw nude models, just to get an idea of the body underneath. The structure. And Mark was one of the sitters. He was picking up extra money. So when I was going over my portfolio—I hadn't even noticed him at the time, I was concentrating so hard—I saw that I had gotten one of them completely wrong. I mean, it was anatomically impossible, what I had drawn. So I freaked out because we had to turn it in. It was going to be our first grade of the class. And I actually tracked him down, through the office that hired people to pose. Just because I wanted him to sit for me again, so I could do it right. And then—"

I stopped. I hadn't ever told this story to anyone before. It was way too personal. And here I was, blathering it out.

"Could you help me?"

I turned around. She was in a party dress, with a zipper in back. It was nice, more expensive than pretty, but too old for her. Almost anything fancy would be. For the first time I realized she was young. She was still at Mark's stage of arrested development, twenty-three or twenty-four. But of course she would keep on growing, while he stayed the same.

"I know what you mean," she said, still facing away from me.

Maybe that's why I was telling her, because she did know what I meant. It was our guilty secret, that we were both helpless before a certain kind of male beauty. When I had drawn him the second time, it was even worse. I could still feel the piece of charcoal crumbling in my hand, making the same mistakes, my mind (or whatever was in control of me, then) twisting reality to its own perverted ends, giving shape to self-destructive desires.

"He still has it."

"Has what?"

"The picture. You gave it to him."

There was a brush on top of a box. She took the rubber band out of each pigtail and shook her hair, giving it the most cursory type of attention, just one or two punishing strokes on either side.

She's so serious, I thought. And with no sense of humor. I couldn't point to any one thing. It was more her manner. A coldness. What was he doing with her?

We made our way back along the wall while I tried to think of something to say. Something like: I didn't give it to him, it just disappeared one day; he must have taken it. Or: Well, as you know then, he's not really that big; I literally *lost perspective.* Or: Give me back my drawing, you jealous cunt. But all I did was troop after her. She was still wearing those ridiculous shoes. She had gotten back into them, after changing. They banged on the wooden floor.

While we'd been gone, Mark had put out bowls and platters of food.

"He got it all wrong," she complained.

"You want me to help?"

"No. I'll do it."

She had a very determined look, storing up credit for some big fight she could have with him now. My offering to help just got him in deeper trouble.

"I guess you didn't want the guacamole on the table saw, huh?"

"Is that your husband?"

She sounded surprised, maybe because Harvey was this normal guy, holding Ann, who was squirming and red-faced. For me, though, he was such a relief to discover, a pillar of stability. And so good-looking, my mind irrelevantly noted.

"Let me introduce you."

But she was already gone, clomping off to move the dips.

"Thank God." He came up and tilted Ann so she rolled into my arms.

"What's wrong?"

"I think she's hungry."

"Are you having a good time?"

"All right." He looked around, confirming what he'd been doing. "I talked to some people."

"Really?"

"I think I'm getting . . . what do you call it, when you're just *around* people who are stoned?"

"A contact high."

"You want a beer?"

"Sure."

He pushed his way toward the refrigerator.

Who are all these people? I wondered. When I knew Mark before, he had no friends, none he'd let me meet. They were all business-related, would show up unannounced, have whispered conversations at the door, then disappear in back, go to the "curing room," a locked closet where he hung bunches of leaves upside down so they dried in a certain way. He kept me apart from all that, which angered me at the time, but also made me feel special. Protected. The people in this new loft were young and hip, by which I meant childless, without any hint of scruffy danger to them. They looked very clean. I found a chair and pushed up my blouse.

"So what have you been up to?" I asked Ann. "Did you go for a ride? Did the man with the funny hair turn you into an airplane?"

I tried moving her into a better position. The one good thing about talking to babies was that you always got in the last word.

"That's what he does. That's his specialty. He makes you fly. Upside down, sometimes."

"I'm in love with your daughter."

Beeswax. I had been wondering what the smell was. I thought it was the plants, at first, but it wasn't. I'd been smelling it ever since we got out of the elevator. Not smelling, really. Breathing it in: the beeswax from his dreadlocks. That all happened when I knew him. He had gone to a Rasta man who showed him how.

He held out a joint.

"I know you are."

"Is it that obvious?"

We touched, lightly. It all seemed so natural. That was the thing about Mark, I remembered now, zeroing in on exactly what it was that made him so attractive. His gift, when you were with him, was how you couldn't make a wrong move. Everything you did felt *right*. I didn't take a hit off the joint. I didn't need to. I just held it. That was enough.

"But why? That's what I can't figure out. Why are you in love with her?"

He bent down and looked, as if her little sucking mouth could provide an answer. One ropy vine of hair bounced against my cheek.

"Because she's beautiful?" he murmured.

"Not much of a reason."

There was music playing. I couldn't pinpoint the source of

everyone's excitement—the old year ending or the new year beginning—just that it was heading toward some kind of peak.

"You met Io."

"Yeah."

"Isn't she great?"

"Great," I echoed.

"She really liked you."

"You already talked to her?"

He nodded. Checked in with her, that was the impression I got. She was his little boss. Well, maybe that's what he needed. A stern taskmaster. I certainly couldn't have filled that job description.

"Look at her go. It's like she's a pump."

"All right, Mark."

I handed the joint back to him. I liked him close to me, part of me did, the part that got me into trouble, but I was too aware of the people around us. Just a second ago, I'd thought some dam was about to break, that all these floodwaters my uptightness walled in were going to run free. But the truth was that when it *had* crumbled, in the past, no magic torrent had been released. I wasn't some free spirit, begging to be liberated, which I knew, but every once in a while forgot and needed to be reminded of.

"I've been meaning to give you this."

He passed me a slip of paper.

"What is it?"

"My number. In case you need to call."

"Should I learn it by heart and then swallow it?"

"Why?"

"Never mind."

He looked around.

"So what do you think of the place?"

"It's big."

"You should come here sometime."

"Yeah?" For some reason that made me laugh, the way things you long to hear often do, when they're actually said out loud. "Come here and . . . ?"

"Just hang out."

I pushed him away. At least that's what I thought I was doing. He always sat too close. A fake clumsiness, I first felt. Then, when I got to know him better, I thought it was a puppylike need for attention. Later still, I decided he was blocking my progress, always right in front of me, in whichever direction I turned. *Move!* I wanted to scream. And finally, one day, he did. He wasn't there anymore. My wish had come true. He was gone. So this time, when I playfully pushed and my fingers found him, they were shocked. They expected to meet air or, at the most, a shirt. Instead, they reached out and pressed against the muscles of his stomach, which were slippery from sweat. They slid in this delicious slick, losing their intelligence, becoming unthinking conduits of feeling, rolling like individual bathers over that narrow arrow that funneled down to his waist. One arm was still holding Ann and the other was having this private orgasm, and he was doing what he did best, which was absolutely nothing, just holding his ground like stone.

"Go away," I said.

"I did." We were having this separate conversation, apart from what was happening. "I am away. Now."

"You think that makes it different?"

"Well." He shrugged. His exquisite naked shoulders. If I had to build a man, I would start with shoulders. "It *is* different. I mean, can't you tell?"

Hand come home, I ordered. For one thing, Ann needed to change sides. She was sucking on empty. It made a strange counterpoint to what I was feeling elsewhere. A pinching, very rhythmically precise, while the other half of me was lost in wet space.

"Mark!"

I blinked. Iolanthe was standing in front of us—

"You put everything out all at once."

—along with Harvey, who held a beer. I took it, switching, so the hand that had been tracing his abdominal development was safely hidden under Ann's warm back. His sweat soaked into her pink terry cloth.

"I know."

He'd obviously heard it before. She just had to say it again, in front of us.

"And now I can't take things away because people are already eating them."

"Well, that's good, isn't it? That they're eating them?"

"You put out the desserts. The desserts are supposed to be for later. They were supposed to be for *after twelve*, remember?"

"Desserts!"

I made it sound like an outrageous unhoped-for treat, trying to smooth the situation over. No one else seemed nervous, though. This was just the way they talked, a low-level aggression. They bickered.

"Iolanthe's studying to become a therapist," Harvey said. "I know the program she's in. It's very good."

"Therapist? I thought you were a—"

"Could you at least *help* me?"

It wasn't a request. It was a direct command, wife to husband.

Harvey moved aside to let him pass, then sat down. It was one of those moments when life gets too symbolic. Boy Toy replaced by Husband. The past by the present. He settled comfortably into the exact same spot, while Iolanthe led Mark off.

"Therapist?" I said. "I thought she was a dancer."

"I'm sure she was. Everyone starts out wanting to be something else. Before reality sets in."

"Really? Did you want to be something else, besides a doctor?"

He thought about it.

"No. I guess I'm the exception that proves the rule."

"And what about me?"

"You're just the exception."

I tore my eyes away from Mark's departing back and looked down. The other hand, feeling shortchanged, was trying to get some relief of its own, squeezing the long-necked beer bottle, doing a rippling caress along its glass shaft. I watched, horrified, as if I had no say in my actions.

"When you're ready, I want you to tell me what's bugging you."

"What if I never am?" I asked, without looking up.

"You will be."

"Might be awhile."

He sat back, a fortress. Very secure and self-contained. Which was nice, if you were inside with him. With the drawbridge pulled up. That's what I couldn't figure anymore: if I was in or out.

"I got time," he said.

　　　•　•　•

If I couldn't make a pilgrimage back to my past, maybe I could make one to my future, I reasoned. And that meant getting a job. Of course it couldn't be a regular job, the kind where they actually expected you to show up at a certain time, be dressed in good clothes, and not bulldoze everyone out of your way with your overloaded stroller. No, it had to be a magic job, perfectly suited to my state of spiritual need.

"Let's go look for Salvation" was how I put it to Ann.

I skirted the park until I found the black rubbery tubes taped down across the sidewalk. The other ends disappeared into a truck that sat with six or seven trailers, all idling, taking up a block's worth of parking spaces. I followed the cables past the entrance, over the ring road, then to the top of a gentle slope looking down on the meadow.

The movie people were huddled at the end of the field, surrounded again by yellow tape. I walked closer, hoping someone would notice, even if it was just to yell at me. I needed to be acknowledged. But the atmosphere was different from last time. They were standing around, sullen and depressed. I couldn't find the director. I stood on my tiptoes and squinted.

"They failed to understand," a voice behind me said.

I turned. He was sitting on a bench, just like a regular person. I must have walked right past him. But he was so small and, like me now, on the outside looking in.

"Few do," he went on. "Look at her."

He motioned to the actress I had seen him with the time before. Two men were crouched around her waist, making some kind of adjustment to her pants, I couldn't see what, except that she didn't like it. She was frowning, getting pulled and pushed by whatever was going on below.

"A simple question of wardrobe. But indicative, naturally, of a much more fundamental failure. I blame myself, first and foremost."

"I'm Eve," I said, finally remembering.

He didn't seem to hear. He looked utterly unmotivated, just sitting, his tiny feet not even touching the ground.

"She is alone in the city." He nodded to the girl again. "She has no one and no *thing*. It is as if she were in hiding. The clothes she chooses make her practically invisible."

"I know what you mean," I risked.

"And yet the trousers they chose to dress her in for this scene are brand-spanking-new designer jeans."

I looked again and saw they were rubbing the legs with sandpaper.

"Can't you just go out and buy some prewashed ones?"

"We haven't the time. And what they are doing now only makes it worse. She looks as if she has been mauled by a Bengal tiger." He shook his head. "But it is more than that. It is not just a question of appearance. It's Jennifer herself. She seems to have lost the vulnerability I once saw in her."

We both watched the rag-doll figure of the actress.

He sighed.

"Have you ever been rolling along, feeling truly inspired, and then the smallest thing, a matter of no real consequence, derails you completely? Reveals the absolute impossibility of ever attaining your goal?"

"Before, you said she was going to have a ray of pure sunshine on her features. That she was going to be Saved."

He blinked. I think it was the first time he actually noticed I was there.

"But that happens later, even though it was filmed earlier. In cinema, we shoot out of sequence."

"So you already know what happens?"

"I suppose I do."

"Wow. Like God, huh?"

"Yes. I am often mistaken for Him. But even He has off days, when all His creation turns to shit."

"I'm sure everything will be OK."

"It would have been better if I had never left the Gramercy Park Hotel this morning," he groaned. "I could be there right now, reveling in the centralized heat."

I took a deep breath.

"Using sandpaper isn't going to work. You have to burn them."

He didn't get it. He was readjusting himself to my presence. But *I* got it. I knew what was happening. It was a miracle. My first, in quite a while.

"You have to burn off the nap. That's how you distress denim. Not by scraping."

Everything was fitting together. Luck. After an unbroken string of disasters—falling in love, getting married, having a child—I was finally catching a major break. If I could only manage not to blow it. If I could only show him I had something to offer.

"See, I took a course at FIT."

"FIT?"

"The Fashion Institute . . . of Technology," I added lamely. "There was a class, I forget what it was called, but we learned all about distressing fabrics and aging them and—"

"Who are you?" he asked, in a completely different tone of voice. "What are you doing here?"

"I told you, I'm Eve."

"Eve who?"

"Just Eve. I came to see if I could maybe get a—"

"Jonathon!"

Everyone on the crew jumped. The one with the clipboard

saw me. He sagged, then started trotting over, ready to boot me out again. The others laughed.

"It's our stalker," I heard someone say.

"Forget it," I muttered, my face turning red.

I turned the stroller around.

"One uses a torch, I assume."

"What?"

"One burns off this nap with a torch, yes?"

"I guess."

It suddenly occurred to me that I could be making this all up. It sounded right, but had I actually seen it done? Had the teacher demonstrated it? I couldn't remember.

"Ma'am." The assistant reached us. "I'm going to have to ask you again to—"

But the director had gotten off the bench. He was full of life now. You could feel the change. In compensation for his stillness, he was moving at twice his normal speed.

"Bring her," he ordered, and strode past us, back into the group.

The assistant must have been used to these mood swings. He grabbed my arm as if I might try to get away.

"I'm fine," I said, trying to free myself.

But he wouldn't let go. He acted like I would have trouble finding my way. He led Ann and me past the table with the food, pointing out cables, guiding us through the crew. People were staring.

"Remember," he counseled, "the key is to do whatever Mr. C says."

"Mr. C?"

He looked surprised. "Martin Cooper. Haven't you heard of him?"

We came to the center of the crowd. The change was complete. The little man was giving orders, drawn up to his full minuscule height, looking like a creature from a fairy tale.

"You will need to disembarrass yourself of that . . . lovely child," he said.

I handed off the stroller to someone who took Ann over to where the muffins were laid out. I could still see her, I consoled myself. And for once she wasn't crying.

"Wait here." Martin Cooper went off to get something.

"We used to have a costumier," the assistant complained, "up until a few days ago."

"What happened to her?"

"He goes through about three a shoot."

I watched Ann from a distance. "Is she going to be OK?"

"She'll be fine."

"Like this?" He returned holding a small propane torch, with the person it belonged to standing behind him.

"Right," I answered, feeling increasingly unsure. "But whoever does it should be careful just to burn off the nap, otherwise—"

"—otherwise the actor herself might be toasted to a crisp, yes?" For the first time, he smiled.

"Oh, you don't do it while the person is wearing the clothes."

"Ideally, no." He took a big silver watch from his pocket. "But we have been out here for almost four hours, and in a few minutes the crew must take its union-mandated break. A trip to wardrobe, and the expense overtime would entail, is simply not in the cards."

"Excuse me," I said, "I don't—"

"I wonder if I could prevail upon you, since you seem afflicted by an almost psychotic propensity for interference, to give us the benefit of your hard-won expertise."

It was as if I had lost the ability to understand my own language.

"I don't get it. You mean you want me to—?"

"Charlie!" He yelled for people even when they were standing right next to him. They didn't exist until he named them. Then he turned back to me. "And you are?"

"I told you twice already. Eve."

"Yes, but Eve who?"

"Nothing. Just Eve."

A brief flicker of annoyance passed over his features but he was very intent on moving forward.

"Light this, will you?"

"Wait—"

"Sure thing, Mr. C."

The equipment man turned the knob up full and pressed one of those electric sparkers until the whole thing exploded. I screamed.

"Ah, now we are making progress. This way, this way."

He was back to his driven self, hurrying us all along. We moved over to where the actress (he kept calling her an *actor,* though) was standing on a spot of grass no different from any other except it was marked by an X spray-painted right on the ground that kept her there, surrounded by hulking equipment. She stared past us, her big blank face completely bored.

"You see the problem."

"Not really," I said.

"Those off-the-rack jeans make her look like some kind of tawdry fashion model, whereas I want her to simply be as battered and defeated as the landscape through which she walks."

"Martin," she whined, "how much longer do I have to stand here?"

"It's quite all right, dear. Now . . . Evelyn?"

"Eve!"

"I want you to, very lightly and delicately, without hurting young Jennifer here in any way, take off the stiffness, the awful coating of newness about her. Can you do that?"

"With her clothes on? No way. She's got to—"

"No one's coming near me with *that* thing," she said, noticing the torch.

"Dear, a moment ago you were complaining about the cold. As you see, I have addressed your concern by finding a Certified Fashion Technician—"

"Oh." She looked impressed.

"—who will not only fix this costume problem that has been holding us up but, I imagine, warm you considerably in the process. It's this area here I'm interested in," he said to me. "Come see."

He knelt down, then went on quietly, right in my ear, so no one else could hear, "It doesn't matter if she cries."

"What?" I asked.

He answered even lower, speaking under the propane's roar, turning to face me, so our eyes really met. His were pale blue. I don't usually notice the color of people's eyes, not right away, but there was something about them that reminded me of certain relationships I'd been in with men whose sole aim in life had been to impose their will. It wasn't the color, but the unblinking quality of the stare that allowed you to *see* the color, really experience it, so it became a dye flowing out and staining your vision, making it a weaker version of their own.

"If she cried a little, it would actually be a good thing."

He raised his eyebrows, implying, You know what I mean, then nodded to the flame, which was still a lazy tongue of white-yellow.

"You don't get it," I mouthed back. "I don't know what I'm doing."

"Ah, but I think you do."

You're wrong, I was about to say. And I was wrong—wrong and crazy—to come here, so find somebody else, when Jennifer, the actor, announced in a pouty, spoiled brat's voice, projecting her speech not at me but into the sky, "If I feel one thing, I'm going to *kick* her."

A few people laughed. I looked up. She was posed there with her knee stuck out. I saw what he meant. She was a mannequin. Stiff. She was also something else, the me of a few years back, shallow and self-absorbed.

"OK," I heard a voice that didn't sound like mine answer, as low and calm as his. "I'll try."

"I want to be ready as soon as she is done," he called, getting back up, leaving me there. "Tony! Frank!"

He started consulting everyone. The spell was broken. There was a jolt of motion. I saw my hand shaking. I reached my other hand out to stop it but instead found the knob and sharpened the flame into a blue cone. It was coming back to me now, not how to do this, specifically, but something more important. I grabbed her inseam.

"Ow!"

"Hold still."

Luckily, they weren't skin-tight. I pulled as much cotton away from her thigh as I could, then concentrated. Once you got up close, the flame had no real border, didn't begin or end. There was an emptiness where the gas came out, before it burned, and at the other end a wavering edge, the hottest point, where the air around it broke up. I sensed, more than saw, each molecule-thin strand of fiber shrivel, lose its sizing in a puff of vapor. Then I moved on. I moved on before it happened. I anticipated. It wasn't just the air that broke up, but the sequence of events. I swept the flame over each bunch of material in broad, even strokes, never pausing.

"I'm going to change sides," I warned, "but you have to stay absolutely still."

Like an animal trainer, I let go and watched her obey me while I crept around, still squatting. I was vaguely aware of people gathered in a circle, and of a light that wasn't there before, hot, on the back of my neck. It wasn't natural, not the sun, but a dazzlingly artificial high noon of electricity that picked out everything and made it exist in a way it never had up until now. For a minute, I didn't know what it was. I thought I was having some kind of mystical experience. Then I realized they had turned on the power, the superbright lamps. They were getting ready.

Costume Design, I remembered. That's what it was called. None of the rich girls had taken it. There was a moment at FIT when you realized it wasn't about fashion at all, about designing clothes that would change people's lives, your own first, then everyone else's. It was about money, either having money to begin with or being so obsessed you would do anything to be admitted into its world of glamour and privilege. That's when you started noticing the types of classes offering preprofessional training. There was Accessories, also known as Bags, Belts, and Shoes; Wholesale Merchandising, which supposedly prepared you to be a buyer for a department store; and Costume Design, for being a costumier, which, I remembered some girls sneering, meant scrabbling around on your hands and knees Scotch-taping the hem of some soap opera actress's dress. Pretty much what I was doing now.

But you're good at it, I argued. That's what you're feeling again, after eight months of being a total incompetent. A sense of craft.

It must have jinxed me, allowing myself that one little pat on the back, because I lingered a second too long and raised a tiny blister on the surface of the denim. It was nothing, really, but high up, where it was hard to get separation. Personally, I thought she overreacted.

"Oh my God!" she screamed. "I'm on fire! Help!"

"Very good." He had been standing behind us for I don't know how long. Now he stepped forward and moved me out of the way.

"Wait," I said. "I'm not finished."

"That's perfectly all right. You have done quite enough. Charlie, if you could disarm Ester, here."

"Eve. But don't you see? There's one more spot. Above the pocket."

Now that I'd got going, I didn't want to stop. But I no longer existed. He brushed past me to comfort Jennifer.

"That fucking murderer you called in," she sobbed. "I thought you said she was certified."

"Yes, she turned out to be an absolute sadist," he agreed.

He pronounced it *sad*-ist, like I was a professional sad person.

"The good news is I think we are ready to begin now. Don't bother cleaning yourself up. You look absolutely stunning. That little accident seems to have helped break through your wall of juvenile reserve."

"I didn't do it because you told me to," I insisted.

"Are we up to speed? Yes? Good. Everyone!"

"Make her cry, I mean."

"Jonathon!"

The assistant reappeared and began leading me away.

"He *told* me it would be OK if—"

"Yeah, he tells people a lot of things."

He wouldn't let go of my arm again.

"What do you mean?"

"Don't worry about it."

"You mean he lied? He was just using me?"

A heartrending wail pierced the frigid air. We had left the magic circle of light. I could feel my regular life returning, with a vengeance.

He looked over to the food table.

"I think your child needs you."

Chapter Five

The cold got worse. I gave up trying to *do* anything and just concentrated on surviving. The chill seemed to be coming from inside my bones. I wrapped myself in a million shawls. Harvey couldn't understand. He didn't feel it.

"And you're better insulated than I am. Women have an extra layer of fat."

"Thanks a lot."

"It's basic anatomy. If we were both in freezing water, I would die first."

"I can't swim," I pointed out. "I'd drown before I froze."

"I'd hold you up."

"Then you'd drown too. I'd pull you under."

"Not if I held you from behind. There's a way to do it. I was a lifeguard for a few summers. I'd hook one arm under your shoulder and across your chest. It's like a hammerlock."

"And what would you do, once you got me in a hammer-lock?"

He thought about it. "Drag you to shore."

"Kicking and screaming."

"In your case, no doubt."

"Did you ever really rescue anyone?"

"I pulled people out of the water. I don't know if they would necessarily have drowned."

We were on the phone, having what I called phone sex, what he called the daily check-in. I don't know how he made the time, he sounded so busy at the hospital, but we managed to talk every afternoon.

"Why are you at Marjorie's?"

"I have to water the plants."

"How long can that take, five minutes?"

"It's something to do."

I watched Ann play on the living room carpet. Marjorie had been gone longer than she planned. Almost a month, now. She'd called twice, apologizing, but not saying why she hadn't come back. Or where she was, it occurred to me later. The second call had been a bad connection, with waves of static rising and falling between us that only I could hear.

"Is there food left? In the refrigerator, I mean."

"No. She left it empty. Which reminds me, what do you want for dinner?"

We talked more. I liked this, the tangled undergrowth of marriage, conversation that wasn't quite pointless but not directed toward any particular goal, more a mutual repair job on each other's psyche, a reminder of why we were together, that our thoughts, or at least our words, could mesh, even if our bodies and feelings temporarily couldn't.

"I have to go."

"I'll see you tonight."

After he hung up, I snooped, more marveling at the organization than looking for clues to what happened. She had left the place in perfect shape. The china was neatly boxed, labeled, and stacked in a corner. It was as if they'd both abandoned the marriage, which was still humming along nicely by itself, without the need for people. I walked through it, fingering wall hangings, picking up figurines. I read the writing underneath, those marks scored on the base.

There was a sound at the door. It set off a burst of happiness in me.

I didn't realize how much I'd miss you, I formed my lips to say, thinking it was Marjorie, finally coming home, and how lucky that I happened to be here.

It kept going, though, a persistent scratching, until I realized it wasn't a key trying to fit in the lock but something more high-pitched and desperate. I picked up Ann and, just as we walked into the hallway, heard this *whumpf* of something heavy landing awkwardly after a bad jump. We got there in time to catch a blur of gray-blue fur, its claws working frantically on the polished wood, trying to get traction before shooting off to the bedroom, to hide under the big queen-size mattress again. I knew the cat was around. I had been changing its litter, putting new food and water in the bowls. But I had never seen him until now.

Not a person coming home, then, but the last shy creature trying to escape.

Fauntleroy, I remembered.

. . .

"Filet mignon." When it came my turn at the butcher's, I tried sounding confident. "One pound."

They were busy. People were jostling, ahead and behind, calling out orders. The weather had turned us all into cavemen needing to cook meat over fire. I didn't think the owner recognized me and was secretly disappointed we weren't going to have one of our joke flirtations, but then, just as he handed me the soft paper-wrapped package, he winked, in the midst of all the chaos, establishing a private line of communication. It was so old-fashioned. I tried remembering if anyone had ever winked at me before. I didn't think so. Or maybe I just never noticed. On the way home, clutching the bag as if he'd given me a dozen roses, I realized he probably winked like that at everyone he didn't have the time to talk to. Every woman. Still, I savored the way it had gone from his eye to mine, then traveled slowly down my spine.

"Your mother's a whore," I giggled, shielding Ann from the cold.

There was a free coupon for soy-based formula in the mail, and since we'd been talking about weaning her but worried about milk allergies I was reading it with real interest, even the little section addressed to MERCHANT, while I balanced her on my suddenly secure shelf of hip and magically selected the right key to get us inside, bags bouncing, cheeks burning. I wasn't even aware of the difference in the apartment until I automatically kicked aside the favorite blanket that I had ripped from her frantically clutching hands and dropped on the floor an hour earlier, right before we left.

It wasn't there.

Or it was, rather, but not where it was supposed to be. It was folded once and then draped over the back of the futon like a decorative little ornament.

The rest of the place looked different too. It was *arranged*. The sliding dump of stuffed animals was a nest now, lining the interior walls of the crib, while her rattles were attached to the higher bars. All the other objects were either picked up or straightened or oriented slightly differently. The floor was visible, for the first time in ages, its yellow pine and geometrical border of light birch and dark cherry. The reason we had taken the apartment in the first place, I remembered, was because of its beautiful floors.

Then I noticed how, off to one side, was a pile of things that didn't fit. A small pillow whose velvet case was so threadbare you could see the dirty white batting pushing out, a broken candlestick, some books with no covers, and, straddling all of them, the biggest item, Ann's swing, with a dead plant I'd been meaning to throw out stuck in its seat.

The Dirt Thief, I thought.

I wrestled Ann out of her snowsuit and deliberately dropped it on the floor. I had to create some clutter. It was too creepy. Because . . . your mess is who you are, I reasoned.

Mindy came out of the kitchen.

"What's this?" she asked.

"It's a cheese grater. Or was. I left it in the microwave by accident and it got kind of melted. But it still works, if you just use that one side."

She put it with the rest of the throw-out pile and went back.

"What are you doing here?" I asked.

Ann was squirming through my arms. I put her down and she immediately cried to be picked up.

"Just tidying."

"Did Harvey tell you to—?"

"Harvey doesn't know I'm here."

"Then how did you get in?"

"The super let me in. I told him I was your sister." She hauled out a huge black plastic garbage bag. "Come. See what I've done."

"I have to go to the bathroom."

The rest of the apartment was still disgusting. Much more so now, by comparison. I couldn't believe how filthy I'd let it get. I closed the door, sat, and noticed mold growing on the shower curtain. Down the hall, I could hear Ann's low-level whine.

"Your mother will be out in a second," Mindy said, as if speaking to a fellow adult, as if I was the child.

When I finished, she was in the living room, sitting in the armchair. I thought I saw her wince slightly at the way I let everything fall, this trail of junk marking my progress, undoing all her work, but she didn't say a word.

"He just let you in?" I asked. "Every time I ask him to do something he acts like he doesn't understand English."

"He doesn't. I speak Spanish. I spent a year in Ecuador."

"What a surprise."

"I told him you were in trouble. That I had come to help you out."

We looked at each other. I was madder at her than I had ever been at anyone in my entire life. I couldn't believe she hadn't already shriveled up and died just from my killer glare.

"You're dripping," she said.

"What?"

She nodded to the package of meat.

"Oh."

I went into the kitchen and almost fell down.

It was . . . I didn't even realize the counters *were* white. I mean, I guess I assumed they had been once, a long time ago, but thought time, age, the tragedy of everyday life, had dulled them to the sooty gray speckle I called a pattern. Now I saw it was just filth, or had been. Instead, there was the powerful odor of cleaning fluid and all these dazzling planes of pure surface.

"You need an apron," she called.

"Why?"

"So your clothes don't get full of grease."

"Aprons are for housewives."

"Isn't that what you are?"

She was standing in the entrance, watching me. I was crouched, trying to make room in the refrigerator.

"What are you *doing* here?" I insisted.

"I wanted to talk to you. Privately. Without one of my bosses looking over my shoulder, making sure I see at least forty patients a day."

"You could have just called."

"It was more a spur-of-the-moment thing."

I gave up and shoved the meat against all the jars, open cans, and containers. I could feel it squish. I should put it on a plate, I thought, if it was dripping, and then saw she was holding one out to me.

"I can't just sit," she explained. "I have to *do.*"

"So while you were waiting for me . . ."

"I started cleaning up. I hope you don't mind."

"This is too weird," I said. "Where's Ann?"

We found her playing in the trash pile, pawing at everything Mindy had designated for throwing out.

She shook her head.

"It's like they instinctively know where they're not supposed to go."

"No. That's just all that you've left for her on the floor," I defended. "Remember, the floor to them is like our . . ." Our what?

I was too dazed to complete my thoughts. "Why throw out the swing, though? It's not broken."

"It's not good for them at this age. Didn't you read the instructions when you first got it?"

"Are you kidding?"

"Let's sit."

She led me back to the chair. Despite what she'd said, it wasn't so different from being in her office. I felt just as uncomfortable.

"Have you thought more about what we discussed last time?"

"Me seeing a shrink, you mean?"

"Or someone."

"No."

"If you don't take care of yourself, who's going to be around to take care of her?"

"Listen, if you're afraid you're going to get sued for malpractice or something, you don't have to worry."

"This isn't a professional call, Eve. You're married to my friend. I thought—"

"And you want me to believe Harvey didn't *ask* you to come here and get me to go see someone?"

"I told you, Harvey doesn't even know I'm here. I'd prefer you didn't tell him about it, either."

"You told Mr. Delgado you were my sister?"

She looked, for the first time, uncomfortable.

"It's my day off."

"So this really isn't about Harvey?"

"What do you mean?"

"Him complaining to you. Last time, you said he was—"

"I said he was *worried* about you. I never said he was complaining." She hesitated. "Have I ever told you the story about Harvey and the old lady?"

"I don't know. I don't think so."

"Once, we were going somewhere in a taxi and, at a light, this elderly lady was crossing the street. She seemed disoriented. So Harvey got out of the car and decided she needed medical attention. He made the cabdriver take us all to the emergency room. We were still in school, then, just students, but we stayed with her for a couple of hours, until her family came."

"I don't get it. What's the point?"

She was looking at Ann. "The point is: Harvey doesn't *complain*. If there's a problem, he tries to fix it. He's one of the most decent men I've ever met."

Ah-hah!

"What were you doing in a taxi?"

Because in my mind *taxi* was right up there with *bordello* in terms of wild promiscuous decadence.

She sighed and got that look, humoring this idiot wife of her friend.

So they just cabbed around the city, like a bunch of comic-book superheroes, looking for citizens in need, never giving a thought to their own raging desires? I felt my heart pounding with indignation. Don't blame me, I wanted to say. I'm sorry if I'm the opposite of everything you'd want for Harvey, if I'm this constant insult to your idea of who he is or what he should be, but if you're even *thinking* about fooling around with my husband, I'll—

"You should talk to him," she said.

"We talk all the time."

"No. I mean really talk."

I stared. "About what?"

"Just . . . talk to him." With an obvious effort, she stared right at me. She looked surprisingly human and embarrassed. "You two should talk."

There it was. Nothing as sensational as, *He's been crying on my shoulder, coming to me behind your back,* or, *He realizes, after less than a year of marriage, what a terrible mistake he's made.* Just this admission, this awkwardness I had forced out of her without even intending to, a secret I could see she had been struggling to keep inside. The real reason she'd come.

* * *

"Wow!" Harvey said, when he got home.

"I know."

"What got into you?"

Your pushy friend. She wants me to change who I am. She wants me to become this second-rate imitation of her. That way she can sit back and watch our marriage with a combination of condescension and approval, instead of feeling that you've betrayed some ideal picture she has of you by . . .

It was too complicated. Instead, I just gave a modest shrug.

"It looks great." He walked around. There was all this extra space to explore. "What's missing?"

"The swing."

"I thought I saw that down by the curb."

"You're not mad, are you?"

"Mad? Are you kidding? I think it's terrific."

"You do?"

"It's like you finally took charge of your life."

Oh, yes, I thought. *That's me. Eve in Charge.*

Later, he wondered why I wasn't coming to bed.

"I will in a minute," I called.

"What are you doing?"

"Writing in that journal."

In fact, I was using it as a sketchbook. I had made lines going down, perpendicular to the ones going across, so each page was a graph, and on that graph I tried plotting just the simplest shapes, painfully dredging up long-buried lessons. The Silhouette. The A-line. I was back to my old dream of designing clothes, clinging to it against this latest assault on my fragile security.

"Really? So you're finding it useful?"

"I guess."

"I thought it might help. Sometimes, when you put things on paper, they make more sense."

"They sure do."

Lying made everything easier, though after the initial falsehood I tried being honest in all the particulars. As long as there was some central act of concealment.

"That was a great dinner."

"Thanks."

"I think you're right. We could start trying the formula. Maybe one bottle a day."

What was it about imagining outfits? I didn't really care about clothes themselves. What I liked was the idea of feeling intensely about something, and fashion, early on, had seemed the most acceptable area to become obsessed with. I liked the process, studying designs, taking them apart and putting them back together, seeing how they worked, how they purred and ticked like those windup watches, the kind with a million tiny gears and springs. But clothes, what they showed in shop windows, I couldn't have cared less about. They seemed symbols of . . . I didn't know what. Greed, maybe. Or stupidity. I hated how much they cost. In every sense of the word.

"Well," he yawned, "I guess I'll turn off the light."

"OK."

"Are you coming to bed?"

"When I'm finished."

The problem was, I didn't have a creative bone in my body. Yes, I liked the idea of making something new, of me doing it, but it wasn't like my pencil now danced magically over the page. All I could do was copy, and—I looked around—there was definitely nothing to copy here in my present life.

An hour later, I came into the bedroom. Harvey was on his belly, a snoring land mass. A continent. I pushed enough of him aside to crawl in.

"You didn't get back here," he murmured.

"What? Oh, you mean cleaning up? No. Not yet."

I listened to his breaths, the even spaces between them.

"I will," I promised, curling up, not at all sure, lying again. "Soon."

• • •

"My mother . . . your *grandmother*"—I forced the word—"would know how to do this. But she never showed me."

We were folding clothes. I had put Ann in one of those carts at the Laundromat. I didn't know what else to do with her. I couldn't use the stroller. I'd had to haul down a week's worth of dirty laundry. Once we got there, it was too cold to leave, so I stuck her in a cart and twirled her around, watching suds. It was another store from before, that's how I was beginning to see them, from when the neighborhood wasn't so trendy. The interior was dark but clean, with an Asian woman keeping her eye on the various machines. Tables were littered with magazines all about TV, what the "daytime stars" were doing.

"You're supposed to button these shirts, I think. I don't know why, though. It's not like there's a person inside."

Harvey had tried getting me to drop them off at the dry cleaners. "They do laundry too," he'd hinted hopefully, but I kept insisting I could take care of everything. It seemed an essential part of my wifely duties. The problem was, I didn't believe in ironing. Irons reminded me of anchors. Or, when you stood them up, tombstones. Besides, what was so bad about wrinkles? They gave clothes character.

"Now ties," I continued wisely, "I have no idea what to do with. So I just roll them up like this, see?"

"You wash tie?" the lady frowned, walking by.

She seemed surprised.

"Once upon a time," I said, "Mommy lived in a place where she wore the same dress, day after day. Everyone did. We all wore the same things, did the same things, and thought the same things, to show that we Belonged."

I stopped. The words felt wrong in my mouth. Did I really want to tell her about trying to live your life as if you were an inhabitant of the Old Testament? Poison her pristine brain? Instead, I had a vision that *wasn't* a memory, at least none I could actually claim to have experienced before. I was a girl again, down by the lake, wading into the water, watching the sky, the way it floated on the surface. I saw clouds and, through them, the sun, which you weren't supposed to ever look at, which could blind you, but now I sensed wasn't as real, as dangerous, as seen when staring straight up. I reached out and touched its reflection, felt it drip through my fingers, not hot or painful but a twinkling essence, bright drops. I splashed them on my face.

"This isn't ours, is it?"

I wiped away tears and concentrated very hard on a piece of clothing left over from someone else's wash. No. It was ours. It was Harvey's underpants. They had turned pink, somehow. Not really pink, more a *pink effect,* I decided, holding them up, trying to appreciate it for what it was. Very subtle. He probably wouldn't even notice, and if he did, so what? It wasn't like anyone else ever saw them besides me.

"You no separate," the woman accused, coming up behind me.

The panels above the dryers were propped open, to heat up the place. You could see into where you weren't supposed to. Blue gas jets licked rotating drums.

"What?"

"Color. Keep color from white. White from color. Don't you know?"

"Of course I know about separating," I said with great dignity. "I just choose not to, that's all."

She gave me a look and swept on by.

"It's an artificial distinction," I explained to Ann. "Mommy doesn't believe in those."

She just took it in. Did she ever blink?

"Your father," I began, but couldn't think of anything to add. Just saying that, "Your father," seemed more of an ending than a beginning.

A voice said, "I thought it was you."

"Oh. Hi."

"Eve, right?"

The woman from the Parallel Play Group, Alison, was standing in front of me. She had just come from outside. She wore one of those knit caps from Tibet that come down over both ears, with each flap ending in a little woolen ball.

"Where's . . . ?"

I tried to remember her kid's name.

"Dominic is with Frances. I needed some time. Looks like you've got a ton of crap here. Are you almost done? Want some help getting it home?"

"That's OK, I—"

But she had already stuffed the last few items in my big bag.

"Come on."

. . .

"So you found all this?"

At first I thought by "all this" she meant Ann, Harvey, the apartment. I was tempted to answer, Yes, I found all this. It was just lying around, waiting to be discovered. Then I realized she meant the clothes I was putting away. Because she remembered me talking about dumpster diving from that disaster time at Osbourne's.

"Most of it." I looked at the closet, which was jammed with items I'd never wear, that I'd never even worn once.

"What about the stuff you sew?"

I had taken out the tailor's dummy. I didn't know why. It was another pathetic gesture, waiting in the corner, accusingly bare, an idol with no offerings.

"No. I never made outfits for me."

"Why not?"

"I don't know. Because it was work, I guess. It would be like mixing business with pleasure."

Alison prowled. She had taken off her coat and hat but wouldn't sit. She had loosely permed hair and rings around her eyes. I couldn't tell if they were from makeup or lack of sleep. I didn't remember her being so intense, that time at the meeting.

"You want coffee?"

"Let's do something," she said. "You want to go somewhere?"

"But I have her."

Ann had passed out on the way home. She was in the crib, with her snowsuit half undone.

"Let's go to Snoopy's."

"That bar, you mean?"

"It's just around the corner."

And up one block, then two blocks over, I added silently.

"I can't."

"Why not?"

"I can't leave her alone."

We hadn't been back more than ten minutes. There were still clean clothes all over the bed. Harvey's underpants looked a lot more pink in the light. I sensed he wasn't going to appreciate them.

"What could happen while you were away?"

"Fire," I recited. "Choking on a toy. Kidnapping. Sudden Infant Death Syndrome."

"You have a baby monitor?"

"Yeah."

Harvey's mother had given it to us. At the time, I thought it was the most ridiculous thing I'd ever seen. Our apartment only had three rooms.

"Plug it in. We'll take it with us. Those things travel over amazing distances."

"No way."

"Come on. Just for fifteen minutes. We'll have a drink. Remember how you used to be able to just go places?"

"What if—"

"Nothing's going to happen. She'll never know you've been gone. And you'll feel so much better."

"Who says I'm feeling bad?"

"I dare you," she said.

"You dare me to leave her and take the baby monitor to a bar?"

"It's a real rush. You'll see."

"So you've done this with Dominic?"

"Once or twice." She came closer and touched my arm. "Come on. It'll be great. I promise."

"Just fifteen minutes?" I asked dubiously.

She was already putting on her coat. Snake hips, I noticed, taking advantage of her eyes being elsewhere, seeing her in terms of a fitting. A body type that doesn't segment. Easy to belt. Because there's nothing really to accentuate or hide. So you can use it more as an ornament. A slash of color. Or a band of metal.

"Wait." I wanted to slow her down. I wasn't even thinking about making a decision. "Let me at least get her out of her snowsuit."

Alison stared out the window. She looked so hard I wondered what was out there that I had missed. Wasn't it just buildings and a tree? Sky above, yes, but not the kind of sky you could look up into. City sky. She bunched what hair she had and pulled it back.

"It's only four," I sighed.

"I know. It gets dark so soon."

That's what she was looking at, her reflection, peering at some new self she imagined.

Because Ann was asleep in the crib, I hadn't turned on any

lights. The room kept its winter feel. Objects were providing their own stubborn illumination, not soaking up sun or sheltering in shade but asserting their existence from within. Everything looked solid and monumental, even my hand, as it drew her out of formlessness—her hot back, her diaper-padded butt, her limp legs—and settled her on top of the covers. I let an extra blanket waft gently down.

"There," I breathed, not quite knowing what I was agreeing to.

"Good."

Alison didn't whisper. She spoke in a normal tone of voice. It was a test. I watched Ann's face, confirming how far away she was already, in her mind. She seemed to be concentrating. Her little brow was furrowed and her lips pursed. Are you troubled? I wanted to ask. So soon? It seemed unfair to already be worried.

Behind me, I could hear Alison moving away from the window.

"Is she down?"

"I guess."

"For at least an hour, right? So let's go."

"I'm not sure I can—"

"Let's *go,* Eve."

She was determined, like we were about to rob a bank.

*   *   *

"I had to burn incense." She pulled at the front of her pants. "Here. Directly over my uterus. I had to burn these sticks, all the way down. See? There's still a mark."

"Who told you to do that?"

"This Chinese herbalist doctor. Don't laugh. It worked."

It never occurred to me to laugh. I was squinting, though, because there wasn't any mark I could see. But then again, I hadn't examined too many women's groins before, certainly not while sitting at a bar.

I had walked by Snoopy's a hundred times, and I had to admit it intrigued me. I was too shy to ever think about going in alone, though. It had TV sets on high shelves over the bottles. Everything was black vinyl: the stools, the booths. It was a nighttime coffee shop, with alcohol taking over from caffeine. Like the butcher's and the Laundromat, it was from before, very old-style and casual. I didn't feel comfortable here. We were outsiders. I caught several people, men and women, looking at Alison.

All right, I thought, stop flashing your gross fishnet panties at me.

"That's not all I had to do. There was this whole feng shui thing. We had a guy come in. It's not just the position but what direction you're facing."

"The direction you're facing?"

"When you do it. You have to be aligned."

"But . . ." I was having trouble following, even though I'd barely touched my drink. I'd asked for white wine and instantly knew it wasn't what I wanted, watching the bartender pour from a big sweaty bottle. "I don't get it. Were you having trouble conceiving?"

"No. But I really got into how you can influence your child's development before it's even born. Did you know there's this theory that a genius is the product of great sex?"

I tried to remember. But how would you even know which time was the one? Unless you were as into consciously arranging things as she was. And anyway, what was great sex? How could you regard it in isolation?

"Does it work with other qualities?"

"Like what?"

"Well, are brave people the result of withstanding painful sex? Are patient people made by sex that takes a long time? Are some people born sneaky because the mother or father was fooling around, cheating on their spouse?"

"Wow," she said. "I forgot. You're really crazy, aren't you?"

"Me?"

The receiving end of the monitor came with a stiff loopy handle so you could hang it off the doorknob or maybe a bedpost. I'd been holding it like a little electronic disco bag. I set it on the bar now, and turned up the volume. A red dot flickered.

"Sorry. I shouldn't have said that. I quit smoking. For Dominic. Sometimes it still gets to me."

"When did you quit?"

"Ten and a half months ago." She looked around. "It's like the way some people don't know what to do with their hands? I don't know what to do with my mouth. Especially at places like this."

I put my ear closer to the speaker, thinking, This isn't going to work. Ann is miles away. Farther than she's ever been. Maybe not geographically, but my being at this bar, with this woman; it was all so alien to my role as a mother. What was I doing here? All these terrible things could be happening. I've got to get home. My legs twitched in reaction to the thought. I could feel the connection stretching, fraying. That word I almost never used, *daughter,* came into my head. I had to go back to my daughter.

"I liked you at that meeting. The way you talked about hating your kid and everything."

"I did not say I hated my kid."

"You were so tense, though. You seem better now. Are you taking something?" She changed the subject without pausing.

"See, I just said I did it for Dominic, quit smoking, but in my own mind I'm not even sure which Dominic I meant. Dominic Senior or Dominic Junior, you know? Because they're both named after each other, kind of. I mean which hatched first, the chicken or the egg?"

"Well if it hatched, then—"

"So sometimes I just say whatever's on my mind. I'm trying to apologize."

"For what?"

"Calling you crazy just now."

I nodded, still bent low, trying to line up my ear with the speaker. The TVs were both going and there was music too. I could hear squeaks and low drawn-out whistles, traces of all those invisible signals that are supposed to be passing through the air.

"Anyway, I liked you," she insisted. "But then you left, really suddenly. And you didn't come to the next meeting. I went, just in case. So when he was driving me absolutely berserk today, I left him with Frances and went for a walk, and then I *saw* you through the window of the Laundromat."

"Who's Frances?"

"You don't know about Frances? She's this woman in the neighborhood who takes care of kids. You can dump them anytime. For only eight dollars an hour."

"You just leave him with a stranger?"

"God, she's saved my life. Once—"

She still had her hat on. I reached out, touched one of the little woolen balls, as if it was a volume control, and squeezed it. To shut her up.

"Oh, Bunny," a voice said.

We both frowned. It was coming from the baby monitor.

The same voice, a woman's, waited a minute, then sighed.

"That's because you don't understand."

She listened, you could feel her, listening patiently, before she went on.

"I know. I know."

"It's a phone call," Alison mouthed, as if the woman could hear us. "You're on someone else's frequency."

"But when I said that, I didn't mean—"

"Why is it only her end?"

"She must be on a portable phone. Sometimes that happens. You hear a conversation, but only half."

"Ladies?" the bartender asked.

We both shook our heads. We didn't want another drink. We were riveted by this overheard talk, waiting for her to answer the silent man on the other end of the line.

"I don't think that," she said, with false decisiveness. She really did think it. You could tell. "It's just that—"

Then he was talking. And talking. And talking.

"Shut up," Alison muttered.

"Bastard," I added.

"No," the woman said.

But he kept on going. Insisting.

"No," she interrupted. "It doesn't matter. None of it matters."

We looked at each other.

"I just want you to come home." She said it not in a weepy way, just a statement of fact. More like he had gone out for a carton of milk. Come home first, was the way I heard it. Come home before . . . I had no idea. I was losing any sense of what this was about. Just that he was drifting away from her.

"All right."

You could feel the balance of their talk had tipped now, that it was wrapping up. It had that speed at the end, when everybody's already said goodbye in their mind. But what had been decided, or left deliberately unresolved, we couldn't tell. It was frustrating. Our faces almost touched, trying to collect the last few bits of sound that came out of the monitor, filtering them from the hundreds of unimportant noises around us.

"I'll— Well, be careful. Well—" She waited. "Of course. You can always—"

"Always what?" Alison snorted.

"Shhh."

We were both holding our breath for her to say, *I love you* or, better yet, *I love you too.*

But nothing followed. Just strange subspace sounds, electronic clicks and squiggles.

"She moved," Alison guessed, after another minute.

We waited some more.

"She must have been in this one little pocket of space where we could hear."

"She didn't even say goodbye," I complained. "And neither did he."

"Whoever he is."

"Bunny," I remembered.

We laughed. I liked Alison at that moment. She was definitely a sideways girl, I decided. She could slip sideways through things, pass from one state to another without seeming to move at all. Sitting next to her, I felt clunky and fixed in place. Chained to my life. I liked her. Maybe because I sensed she liked me. Then, all at once, her face darkened.

"Shit."

"What?"

"I should go."

"Why? Can't we have another drink?"

"It's almost five. I told Frances I was just going out to shop. That was three hours ago."

"So? Does she have to be someplace?"

"Her? No, she's there forever. But Dominic will be home soon and—"

She was discovering all these new thoughts. Not liking them. "And what?"

"I really did have to go shopping. There's nothing in the refrigerator. But I don't have time now."

She was off her stool, leaving the bar. I grabbed the baby monitor and followed. By the time I caught up with Alison she was already out the door.

"Slow down," I called.

She was stalking down the street. From behind, I could see her sashaying like a demented runway model. By the time I caught up, her hands were compulsively smoothing the front of her coat, as if it was covered with crumbs.

"I got to get my story straight," she muttered.

"What story?"

"Exactly."

"What are you talking about?"

"What I've been doing this whole time."

I was aware of Ann again, that I had left her. We were coming to a corner where I would have to turn to get back to our building and I was afraid Alison would walk straight. I couldn't leave her so freaked out. I put on a burst of speed, to get slightly ahead, and took her elbow.

"Everything's fine."

"For you, maybe."

She looked down at my hand but didn't shake it off. I turned us both, so we were heading for home. I needed her company as much as she needed mine. Maybe more. I tried not to panic, sensing that the closer we got, the higher the likelihood something had gone horribly wrong. My mere absence, now that I had abandoned Ann for that first crucial time, no doubt triggered some disaster waiting all these months to happen.

"It's just so screwed up," she said. I could feel her body go jaunty, the way it was before, slouching on her bar stool, her other mode, besides miserable and wired. "I feel like I'm Under Suspicion. You know what I mean? And when I do manage to get away, it's like I'm on some work-release program from the local jail."

"Can't you do takeout?"

"Takeout." She nodded. "Absolutely. Great idea."

We had stopped. We were standing in front of the building. I didn't make a move for the door, though. I was terrified of what I'd find.

Alison put up her collar, trying to stay warm.

"Pretty weird," I began.

"She sounded like an idiot."

Our exchanges were tiny tropical islands, bits of palm tree and coral that made it above the waves, more important for the distance they embraced, the unspoken ocean.

"No, she didn't," I said. "I thought she sounded like . . ."

"Me?"

"Like *me*, actually."

She nodded. Yes. It could be both of us. One didn't exclude the other.

"And we're not idiots," I concluded. "Are we?"

"I got to get my story straight," she repeated, took my face between her hands and without any warning stuck her tongue—

she'd had a beer—between my lips, this wet alien shove. We stayed that way for about ten seconds, then she sucked back, taking half of me with her, and was gone, hurrying down the street.

Something was happening in the air all around me, but I couldn't figure out what.

I got out my keys. Dropped them. Picked them up. I tried putting the mailbox key in the front door. Finally, I found one that fit and went inside.

The laundry, I thought, as a way of covering my anxiety during what felt like the endless flights of stairs. I have to put away the laundry.

Ann was exactly as I'd left her. I lingered, still with my coat on, listening to her breathe, taking in the contrast between her dainty sips of air and my frantic panting.

"Sorry," I whispered, and then thought, What are you apologizing for? She doesn't even know you left.

I swallowed the taste in my mouth—no, not a taste, a feeling, the pressure, the surprise, the invasion—and resolutely returned to the business of sorting. The underwear was definitely going to be a problem. And there was one rogue sock. There always is. I held it up, trying to decide if it was mine and didn't match, if I had lost its mate, or if it was someone else's I had ended up with by mistake.

"Jesus Christ, you kissed a girl!" I said.

That's when I looked out the window and saw it was snowing.

Chapter Six

The flyers appeared overnight. There must have been at least fifty, tacked or taped to every surface, wrapped halfway around light poles, plastered to the back of WALK/DONT WALK signs, crowding out announcements on community bulletin boards:

MISSING CHILDREN

The pictures were terrible. There was another baby next to Alex, but cut off, half a face, a mitten, an arm. Ian was on a rug, in just diapers, dwarfed by furniture, his eyes bright red. It was strange, seeing them apart, with different backgrounds, in photos taken at different times. They were such a pair. I knew which was which now, or thought I did, even though they hadn't been around in so long.

At first it made no sense. Ian and Alex weren't missing. They were with Marjorie. And the number it said to call "with information" was in Manhattan. Marjorie lived in Brooklyn. By the third sign, I began looking for her, imagining I might be able to spot her just outside the camera's range, where the Plexiglas of the bus shelter began, or in the wooden planks of the bin used to disguise a restaurant's garbage cans. Then I realized it was Sherman, of course, taking the pictures, on one of his weekends with the kids, and the phone number must be for his new place, the apartment he had moved into.

But why?

I removed one carefully, trying not to rip the edges, and held it in front of me as I walked.

Missing children?

I crumpled it into a ball. It was about the divorce, of course. About custody. I turned, meaning to go back and get the other two I'd seen, do the same to them, then stopped and instead looked around to see if anyone was watching. I felt guilt by association, as if I had broken the law just by taking down a piece of paper, and fear, that it could be used against me as evidence. Evidence of what, though? That I knew a woman who had run off with her kids? That I was helping her, by watering her plants and feeding her cat?

I didn't have Ann. Harvey had her for the day again. He insisted.

If they wanted to take her away from me, declare me an Unfit Mother, fine. I walked on, imagining I was half Marjorie, half myself, combining our situations, meeting society's disapproval with my head held high. It was perfect, in a way. Mindy was a pediatrician. Medical school sweethearts, this ready-made baby, a birth mother who kept saying how much she didn't love her child. Had I said that? It seized me, the panic of that possibility. Had I ever said, out loud, that I didn't love Ann?

By now, I knew better than to use my free day trying to have a "good time." Instead I assigned myself a million chores. I'd even made a list. First was Clean Rest of Apartment, but I knew I wasn't really going to do that. Not yet. Just writing it down left me exhausted. Second was Exercise, which was another joke, something Harvey had been hounding me to do. Join a gym. Then there were small things, ten or fifteen, that didn't seem so bad individually, but put together added up to an overwhelming case of paralysis.

MISSING CHILDREN

The signs were everywhere. I had to get away. Each one of them was an accusation, a threat, a prediction. They began to look slightly different, even though I knew they were all the same. If I put them all together, in some sort of order, they would tell a story, which was impossible, wasn't it? I walked faster, picked my way through shoveled paths, broke the surface of the frozen-over slush, felt my face freeze into a mask.

There was something else I had meant to put on my To Do list, something important—the entire reason, in fact, that I had gone out—but I couldn't remember what. It haunted me. Which was so typical. Some looming omission that made everything else pointless and trivial.

Grace would come to us individually. That's how it was always put at the Colony. You would be surprised. Surprise was an important element. If you tried making Salvation happen, you were in control and, of course, control was the last thing Grace implied. It was all about giving up. Giving yourself over. Service and Bible Study were preparation so that, when the moment came, you would be ready to receive. You wouldn't let it flash by. Most people's minds were flabby, we were taught. Ours had to be kept in "peak spiritual condition." I smiled, thinking that was the kind of gym I should be looking for. Except it wouldn't be a gym, of course. And it wouldn't be a church either. What would it be?

By this time, I had trudged past the unofficial end of the neighborhood. There were no more signs for Marjorie's children. Or for Personal Fitness Instructor. Or to Learn Portuguese from a Native Brazilian. Row houses instead of brownstones stretched away at each corner. Their fronts were shingle or cheap siding. They had spindly metal banisters and wooden steps, not stoops of poured cement. A few blocks later, I stopped in front of an empty store window. All it displayed were dustballs, a take-out coffee cup lying on its side, and a pair of scissors. I squinted beyond the emptiness and saw fabric. It was a sewing supply store. I couldn't remember walking by it before. It would have been easy to miss. There was no sign overhead. The door had that old-fashioned handle you gripped with four fingers and pressed with your thumb. I stepped inside. A bell barely tinkled.

"Hello?" I called.

It had been a long time since I walked between rows piled high with bolts of cloth. I used to know all the stores on the Lower East Side. My specialty was remnants, finding a way to coax the last thread of fabric from what was essentially just a scrap. That's how I made my money, what little I did, not from labor. I worked more hours than I charged for. I couldn't let go.

Remembering, I walked deeper into the silence.

Bolts were the ultimate luxury. All that pattern unfolding in wide sections, going on forever. I pulled one out, just to feel the weight of it, the texture and smell. I slid the material back in and took out another. They stacked so high, like books in a library, shutting out what weak winter light shone through the bare window. Of all the stores I'd found, this felt the oldest. The air was soft and undisturbed; the floor was ancient. There was a unity of purpose modern places didn't believe in, nothing but fabric from floor to ceiling, except at the cash register, where the ripping station waited, the smooth worn board marked off in inches and feet, with cheap accessories hung on the wall behind, buttons, elastic, needles, thread.

I felt the familiar urge to work again. To make something. But what?

"You can go screw yourself!" a man's voice shouted.

I jumped and looked behind me. There was still no one, just the silent rows, with all those white rectangles, the stiff core each bolt of cloth was carefully wound around, sticking out at slightly different lengths, the sawed-off ends of bones. The sound was coming from the back room, past a curtain.

"That is *not* what I said. . . . No. No, you listen to *me*."

Someone was on the phone. It was the other end of the conversation. It was the man speaking to the woman Alison and I had overheard at the bar.

I reached down and dug my fingers into the nearest pile.

"See, you twist everything," he complained. "All I meant was—"

I tried connecting his anger to her soft, reasonable pleading, and then thought, Eve, wait a minute, you're going nuts.

"Look, we can't do this anymore."

Is this how people really talk? I wondered. When you only heard one half of a conversation, it came across not as an exchange of information or ideas or feelings but two solitary prisoners slugging away at their own tired obsessions.

"I don't give a shit!" he screamed.

I tried concentrating on the hundreds of bolts, on the soft light. I wanted to drown out what I was hearing. It was so ugly. But I couldn't leave. It would make the bell tinkle again. It would alert the man back there to my presence. He would know I existed and I didn't want that. I wanted to stay invisible, surrounded by yards and yards of whole cloth, a still perfectly unformed person. Then I saw a piece of fabric neatly folded into a square. It lay at the end of the counter, right next to the door.

"All right." He laughed in a cynical way. Nothing mattered anymore. "Whatever you say."

My hands clutched at my chest, where Ann would have been if I had her in the Snugli. I was more alone now, with her taken away, than I had ever been before she existed.

"See you tonight."

His voice had changed. Something was happening but I couldn't understand what. The unseen Hand had turned the knob again. Everything shifted.

"Yeah. OK. Hey . . ."

He started telling her something he'd forgotten, not wanting to say goodbye. He was affectionate. Loving. That horrified me more than the fighting. It had become your typical marriage talk, what Harvey and I did on the phone every afternoon at one. I was wrong. It wasn't some horrible fight, a hopeless relationship. It was an ongoing thing. It was just . . . life. Just the irritation of constant contact.

I made my way to the door, drawing in my shoulders. Suddenly, I wanted out just as badly as, a moment before, I had wanted in. The square of fabric was hanging slightly over the edge of the counter, waiting to be picked up, trying to escape. Take me with you, it said. Without thinking, I grabbed it, rescued it, stuffed it into my coat pocket. Then I pushed down on the little metal tongue and pulled back the thick plate glass just enough to squeeze through. The bell made one strangled *clink*.

"Hold on a sec, someone's here."

I tore the door open the rest of the way and left, hurrying down the sidewalk, terrified at what I had just done. My ears were straining to hear the door open, the bell ring, waiting for him to yell, "Stop, thief!" But how could he know it was me, as long as I didn't run?

Act normal, I told myself, fighting the urge to look back. Act normal. Act normal. Act normal.

* * *

"Why?" Harvey asked that evening, when I tried describing what happened. "Why did you do that?"

I had never seen him so annoyed. It seemed out of proportion to what I had said. I thought he would find it funny.

"Never mind."

Well, not funny. I decided to tell him because I was tired of keeping things from him. I missed his ability to comfort me. That's what I needed, comfort. But this time all he did was frown and look around the restaurant as if someone might be listening.

"I mean you go into a place, a guy's talking on the phone, you listen to his private conversation, then grab something that doesn't belong to you, and take off. What's that *about*, Eve?"

"I have no idea. Can I have some more wine?"

"Your glass is still full."

"Oh. Sorry." I picked it up and drank about half.

"Wait. Shouldn't we toast?"

"Oops. Sorry again."

He raised his glass. "Happy anniversary."

"Happy anniversary," I toasted solemnly and drank the rest. "Now can I have some more wine?"

That, of course, was what I'd meant to put on my list: **Buy Anniversary Present.**

I'd remembered, as recently as the night before. I'd known about it right up until the actual day. The fact that I'd forgotten, I took as a bad omen. Did that mean I wished it had never happened? Not that our wedding had been a particularly memorable event. I was four months pregnant. Harvey was deep into his residency. We'd had to grab witnesses from the other couples waiting at City Hall.

He must have known I'd forgotten. It was definitely a hostile act that he hadn't managed to mention it, in passing, that morning, so I could have at least acted like I knew. Instead he treated it as a surprise, with roses waiting for me, and a babysitter, our first, all lined up.

"I'm sorry it's been so rough for you. This year."

"Don't be silly." I was determined to make the evening work, even though we'd gotten off to a bad start. "I like rough."

"What do you mean?"

"I don't know. You keep asking that: What? What do I mean? I don't know what I mean until I say it. And then it's too late. Then I have to figure it out the same as you. I mean, do you consciously *think* about what you're going to *express* and then *translate* it into words, that come *out of your mouth*?"

He thought about it. "Yeah. Pretty much."

"Oh."

It was a beautiful restaurant. I had never seen so many fresh flowers. If I had known we were going out, I could have thought about what to wear, instead of having to grab the first, most deeply inappropriate thing I could come up with, changing out of that at the last minute into something just as bad but wrong in the other direction, too prissy and formal, then taking half of that off, while he was already standing at the door looking at his watch, and ending up wearing an absurd mixture of the two.

"You look good," he said.

"I need a haircut."

We held hands on the soft white tablecloth.

"I guess what I was trying to say," I sighed, "is that when things are rough, at least you know you're alive. Who wants things to be easy? Then you're just sliding along. You have to have a little resistance, a little texture to your life. So you can feel it happening."

"Still, it's been a difficult year for you."

Why was he so into getting me to admit how miserable I was?

The whole ride in, I had been wondering what I should say. That I ordered a present but it hadn't arrived yet? Or tell the truth, that I couldn't find anything? That he was impossible to buy for? That every attempt I'd made at accomplishing anything these past few months had been a dismal failure? I even imagined a third scenario of getting up, sneaking out of the restaurant, trying to find a store, any store still open at night, and—

"It's not over yet," I said.

"What isn't?"

"The year."

"Well." He looked confused. "Yes, it is. That's why we're here. Because it's been a year."

"Oh. Right. I was thinking of something else."

"Of what?"

"Never mind."

In my mind, the year he was talking about was the year we hadn't had sex. The anniversary of our wedding, what was that? Just some artificial date. It's not like anything had *happened.* Suddenly, I knew what I should give him: me. Wrapped up with a ribbon and a bow, if necessary. It must have been in the back of my head before I consciously realized it, because, looking down, I saw that I was very conveniently dressed like a prostitute. I stopped—the idea physically arrested me—and smiled down into my wineglass.

"What?"

"Nothing."

I found his foot, under the table.

"She's only sixteen." He was talking about the babysitter. "But her mother said she's taken care of small children before. She has the number of the restaurant, just in case anything happens."

"I'm sure she'll be fine."

I wanted to reach across and ruffle not just his hair but his whole face, chase the worry from it. I loved its worn quality, so broken in, the expressions that passed over it, his eyes, his mouth, so human and caring. A wave of love lifted me out of my chair.

But he didn't feel any of this. He didn't even seem to notice my foot. He was troubled, gearing himself up for a big announcement.

"There's something you should know."

"No, there isn't."

I sensed immediately that this was wrong. What could he have to tell me?

"Yes. There is."

"I really don't like knowing things."

"It's important, Eve. It's something that's been on my mind for a long time."

I tried to figure out, from his tortured look, what was coming.

"Something's been happening. Something's been going on that you weren't aware of."

Then it hit me.

Oh God, he was going to tell me about Mindy. Whatever it was that existed between them. He was going to blow it in that earnest, disastrous way of his. Get everything out in the open. Just when I was beginning to feel so good about us again. What he didn't get was how I didn't want to know. I wanted a fresh start. I wanted this whole time in our lives to be a set of dirty clothes we would now slip out of, leave heaped on the ground, and walk away from. I wanted our relationship to be based solely on what happened from this moment forward.

"I haven't been entirely truthful with you."

To stop him, I'd worked my stockinged foot out of my shoe and twined it halfway up his leg.

Just shut up, I tried to convey, pressing against his inner thigh. Don't tell me another thing.

"The more I think about it, the more I see it's the cause of all the problems we've been having lately. Why we haven't been able to really talk the way we used to. And it's my fault." He shook his head. "It's why I got in such a bad mood with you a minute ago. I feel so responsible for what you've been going through. Your unhappiness."

"I'm not unhappy, I—"

"Then, to cover it up, I get guilty and angry."

Do I have to actually make you come with my big toe? I tried threatening. Is that what it's going to take to head off this train wreck of a confession you seem headed for? Because I'll do it. I'll do anything not to hear—

"Eve."

He stopped my foot with his hand. His fingers closed over the inside of the arch and squeezed. It was just like that first time, in the clinic. Tears welled in my eyes.

"Stop it!" I said. "I know about you and her, OK? And it doesn't matter. I mean, I don't want to know how far it went. I just hope she wasn't charging us, that's all. If she got to have sex with you, in return for all those stupid baby checkups, that's fine, I guess. It's like the barter system. That should have been enough, though. She shouldn't have been paid too. In addition."

I didn't know what I was saying. It *barely* made sense, although I trusted the emotion behind it, but mostly what it did was stop him from talking. If this horrible topic was going to come up for discussion, despite all my efforts, I wanted it at least to be on my terms. I didn't want to be told. I wanted to show him I knew all along.

"What?" he asked.

"Will you stop saying *What?* Everything I say, you say, What? What? What? Like I'm . . . I don't know . . . unintelligibibibble."

He let my foot go. It slid to the floor with a thump.

"You know about me and—?"

"Mindy! I saw you and Mindy together. That first day you took Ann. By yourself, supposedly. So I could have 'fun,' remember? I saw you kiss her."

"You saw me kiss Mindy?"

"On the cheek."

"I was probably just saying goodbye."

"And I saw the look you gave her."

"What look?"

"The kind of look you used to give me."

Our food came, which of course even heightened the tension more. The waiter hovered around us.

"More wine?"

"Thank you," I said.

"Fresh pepper?"

"Why not?"

I kept my head down, knowing Harvey was about to burst, and listened to the twist of the grinder, the waiter's footsteps going away, then that moment of silence in between, that decent interval before you could start talking again. One, two, three . . .

"There's nothing going on between Mindy and me. We're just friends. Jesus! Are you out of your mind?"

"Is this what I ordered?" I frowned, finally looking up.

"Yes."

"So you're saying it was a hallucination, when I saw you two together that night?"

"We were running late. We were coming back from the doctor's."

"What do you mean, coming back from the doctor's? You *are* the doctors!"

"Stop shouting."

"I'm not—"

He reached out again. My hand had a fork in it. He covered it, fork and all, like when you put a tent over a canary cage. To make it go to sleep.

"We took Ann to a pediatric oncologist because she had a

growth on her finger," he said, in a low, serious voice. "The doctor ordered an X ray. He got the results back, and they're negative. We had a follow-up visit today and she's fine."

He took his hand back. I stared at what he'd left me, four fingers, a thumb, a bar of metal lying across.

"Mindy noticed something," he went on. "At one of those checkups. A growth."

"Above the knuckle," I said automatically.

"Right. She called me, and we decided that, in your condition, with all the uncertainty about what it could be—" He stopped and started over. "It was nothing. We were both ninety-five percent sure it was nothing. But we didn't want to put you through the waiting."

"We?"

"I made an appointment and took Ann there on that day off I gave you."

"What about her?"

"Mindy volunteered to come. To keep me company."

"Just like old times, huh?"

"We're not sleeping together, Ann. We never were. I told you, we're friends."

I looked up. "Ann? I'm not Ann."

"Eve," he corrected. "You've been acting like such a basket case lately that I was worried this would push you over the edge. But I was wrong, all right? Clearly you've sensed that something was up. Mindy said she went over to see you the other day, and—"

"So that's why she came."

"—she felt I should talk to you."

"So you're not sleeping with her?"

I tried keeping the note of disappointment from my voice.

That would be so much simpler an offense than what he seemed to be telling me, which was this deep and horrible betrayal.

"Of course I'm not sleeping with her."

"Then who *are* you sleeping with?"

"No one." He thought about it a minute, and then repeated, allowing himself to sound a little aggrieved, the only time he had ever complained, "I'm not sleeping with *anyone.* You know that."

Our main courses had just been sitting there, getting cold. He took a mouthful, to avoid my glare.

I had ordered meat, but there was no way I could chew. All my bones had dissolved. I tried acquainting myself with what felt like a new world.

"So Ann's sick?"

"No. She's *not* sick. That's what I'm trying to tell you. She had an abnormal growth on her finger, which, in very rare cases, can become a sarcoma, a kind of cancer. But with her it's just a cyst. Probably from sucking on it."

"A teething bump."

He nodded.

"The doctor said it should go away all by itself."

He had called me Ann. We were both children to him, people to take care of. Patients.

"Everything all right?" the waiter asked.

"Very good," Harvey mumbled.

"Delicious," I said.

Delicious, but I have just decided to become a vegetarian. I lifted my wineglass instead.

"I'm sorry, Eve. I made such an obvious mistake." He was beating himself up, so I wouldn't. Getting in ahead of me. "It's like a medical history I remember studying in school. A woman was complaining of acute neuralgia, a pain in her side that seemed to be psychosomatic. So the doctor tried to hypnotize her. And at first it worked. The pain went away. But then she started vomiting, having headaches."

"I don't have—"

"The point is: You can't just treat the symptoms." He was lecturing, like I was the one who needed to learn the lesson. "You have to deal with the underlying causes, otherwise it manifests itself somewhere else. I thought, if I just removed things from your life that made you anxious, you would feel better. But instead you're going around imagining all sorts of crazy sexual liaisons. Not to mention stealing fabric."

"What happened to her?"

"Who?"

"The woman in the story. What was wrong with her to begin with?"

"That's not the point."

"I know it's not the point, but—"

"She was raped," he said, in a reluctant, offhand way.

I laughed.

"Are you going to eat yours?"

"I don't think so."

"You want something else?"

"No."

"You want to leave?"

We were still married. That's what was so amazing. Everything was superficially the same. He took a few bites and, in between, shot me anxious looks.

"I'm not going to make a scene, if that's what you're worried about."

"You have every right to be mad, but don't let that get in the way of the fact that there's genuine good news here. Ann's OK."

"I never knew she wasn't."

"You must have sensed it."

"No. I didn't. I don't have feminine intuition or maternal instinct or any of that crap. I thought maybe you two were fooling around. And then when she told me to talk to you, I was sure of it."

"But if we'd told you straight out—"

"I'm good in emergencies, Harvey. It's the boredom I'm having trouble taking. You stole something from me. You stole something from *us*. It would have been an ordeal in our life we could have gone through together. It would have brought us closer."

He hung his head. I could see his bald spot. So many years ago, when he was a newborn, there had been that soft, skulless way in to who he was. And now, was there nothing left but a shut door?

"I knew, almost immediately, it was the wrong thing to do," he sighed. "But I didn't know how to get out of it. The worst part was not being able to talk. I've missed you so much. Missed you when you were right in front of me. When you've been in my arms."

I never realized how, in the past few months, I had come to depend on Harvey as this judge-on-high of right and wrong. He was my moral compass. He was busy being good, so I didn't have to. And of course you can't sleep with someone like that. You can only admire him. If he'd started to treat me more and more as a child since Ann was born, until he couldn't even tell us apart in terms of helplessness, I had done the same, turned him into just as much of an object, a statue of strength and wisdom.

"What do you know about the bathrooms here?" I asked slowly.

"Why? Are you going to be sick? You shouldn't drink so much if you're not going to eat."

"No, it's just that usually restaurants like this have really fancy bathrooms, whole rooms. For one person at a time."

"Go ahead. I'll tell them you weren't feeling well. We can take all this home, if you want."

"With doors," I went on, "that lock."

I put my foot inside his pant leg this time, as far as it would go. For the smartest person I knew, Harvey could be incredibly slow. It was like trying to pry a boulder loose and push it down a hill. Of course, once you got him rolling . . .

"Eve," he said, "I don't think we can—"

"Why don't we make it a new anniversary? Or whatever comes before the anniversary. The thing you were happy about in the first place. Let's go back to that, the actual event, instead of just remembering."

"That doesn't really work. It's still our anniversary, no matter what. You can't change history. I mean, it's still the date we got married on."

"I want to do it in the bathroom, Harvey."

"Yes, I figured that out. But I don't see how. We can't both get up at the same time and—"

"I'll go first, then you wait a minute. Just knock. Remember, it's the Ladies' Room, not the Men's Room. That's very important."

I could see he was intensely uncomfortable.

"This isn't really my thing."

"I know. That's why we're going to do it."

"What if a waiter comes?"

"If a waiter comes he'll refold our napkins. I've been watching him do it on the other tables."

"All those other people aren't off having sex in the bathroom."

"Maybe they are. Who knows? Who cares about other people?"

We were staring at each other.

He ran his hand through his hair, nervous. "If I go along with this, does it get me just a little bit out from under what I did?"

"Just a little."

"How much?"

"That depends."

I took my foot away. We were magnetized. I could feel the pull, that clean metal-to-metal attraction. I was angry at him, so angry the emotion was a pure force that could be used for anything, put to any purpose, so angry that, if I wasn't careful, we were going to end up making a furious genius.

"Dr. Gabriel?"

A waiter was coming over.

"Could you tell me where the Ladies' Room is?" I asked sweetly.

"Certainly, madame. Just past those flowers, on your right." He turned back to Harvey. "There's a phone call for you, doctor."

We frowned.

"Are you on call?"

"No. And even if it was an emergency, I have my beeper."

"Well, tell whoever it is you can't talk to them right now because you're about to go off and get—"

"I'll be right there," he told the waiter.

I watched while he went over to the little podium at the front of the restaurant. I still couldn't believe what he'd done, that he'd *kept* something like that from me. I wondered just how helpless and neurotic I must have been acting for him to do it. A basket case, he'd called me. Had I been that bad? We needed to get back together again, on the most basic level. If he would just get off the stupid phone. Who could be calling? Who even had this number? Nobody but the babysitter.

I looked over and saw his expression. Something was wrong. Immediately I thought of Ann. He was pale, speaking very quickly. It wasn't paranoia anymore. I was through with paranoia. This was the real tragedy all the paranoia, all the false anxiety, had been in preparation for. A cold breeze blew through me. My knees shook. Quick, think of something else. "Madame." The waiter had called me Madame. That was better than Ma'am, certainly, or Mother, or Mrs. Or Ms. Or Miss. It had a kind of warrior sound to it. Madame. But it still wasn't me. I stared down at the grease forming on my lamb chop until I couldn't take it anymore. I stood up to join him. He was just hanging up when I got there.

"What is it?" I asked. "Did something happen?"

His face had a look of concentration, like he was trying to solve a math problem.

"Harvey, that was the babysitter, wasn't it? Is Ann OK?"

"Ann's fine," he said.

"Oh, thank God. I was sure that—"

"It's my mother."

"Your mother?"

"She had a heart attack. The neighbor found her."

"Is she all right?"

There was a big snifter of matchbooks by the phone, each with the name of the restaurant on the cover. He picked one up, then opened it, to look at the matches on the inside. I could see him shrinking, going away, inside his skin.

● ● ●

We took a cab home. I thought about the story Mindy told me, the old woman crossing the street in front of them. I wanted to hear his version, but it didn't seem the right time to ask. We held hands for a while. Then the cab went over a pothole and they bounced apart.

"I have to talk to my Attending."

"About getting time off?"

He nodded. "There's the body to claim and the room to clean out."

"Isn't there anyone else who can help?"

"It was just us."

I hadn't really known Arlene. There seemed to be plenty of time for that. She missed our wedding, it was on such short notice. We talked, on the phone. She was like Harvey, that's how I instantly saw her, that same reserve. I could tell we weren't going to be bosom buddies, sharing confidences or anything like that. But she trusted his judgment and she wasn't mean to me, which, considering I was knocked up when we got married, she certainly could have been. She accepted me, for his sake. I racked my brain to think of one moment we might have had. When Ann was born I called her, and she was pleased, but it was just an interlude before she asked to speak to Harvey. Then she had come up to visit. They clearly had something intense. I didn't want to meddle, get between them. His father had died a while back, but even before then it was obvious they had spent all this formative time together. There were no sisters or brothers. Once, I'd said to him, "So we're both only children," and for a minute it looked like he was about to object. He wasn't alone like me, I could tell he wanted to say. He had her.

And now she was gone. It was crazy. Maybe I did have feminine intuition. Hadn't I been sensing this whole time that something bad was going to happen? I just didn't know what.

"There's probably some special kid seat that we have to request, when we make the reservations. The kind you use in a car. Or maybe we just have to buy one, I don't know."

He blinked, drawn up, like a well bucket, from some deep place.

"We?"

"Ann and me."

"You're not coming."

"To Florida? Of course we are."

He turned away. We were stuck at a light, waiting to get onto the bridge.

"That isn't necessary."

"You don't want us to come?"

"You'd be . . ."

"More trouble than we're worth?"

"No. It just doesn't make sense."

"It makes perfect sense to me."

"I do these things better alone."

"What, feel?"

The night was crawling over his face. Poor sad—but then I went on, I couldn't help it—*stupid* man. Turning down what was clearly so right for him. What the sensible part of his brain knew he needed. We weren't as different as we pretended, really, both recognizing, in the other, salvation, but also determined, as soon as we stopped concentrating, to screw it up.

"I'm coming with you," I said.

"You'd be bored. And having her there, without all our equipment—"

"I'm coming with you."

"Suit yourself."

He yawned and put his arm around me. I sank into his side.

But the next morning, morning starting officially at 1 A.M., Ann got sick. It was a bad joke, considering how much time he had spent, at dinner, convincing me she was healthy. He found a flashlight and played it over the side of her red, screaming face. Then he burrowed in deeper.

"It's nothing. She has an ear infection."

"Nothing! Then what's all this white vomit about?"

"It's partially digested milk."

"And that's supposed to make me feel better? Now that you've lied to me once, what's to prevent you from lying to me about her all the time? How do I know she doesn't have a brain tumor?"

"She does not have a brain tumor. Vomiting is often the result of intense pain."

"So she's in intense pain? And I'm supposed to just sit here?"

"The Tylenol should take care of that. Then, tomorrow, or this morning, whatever this is, you have to take her in to Mindy and—"

I stopped him with a look.

"All right. No Mindy. Never mind. I'll write you a prescription for antibiotics."

"But we can still go with you, right?"

He shook his head.

"She can't fly."

"Why not?"

"The cabin pressure could rupture her eardrum."

"Then we'll leave her here. We'll rent a cow. And put a pile of hay between the crib and the wall, so when it goes to eat, its udders will be directly over her. That way, all she has to do is—"

"Eve."

He knelt down, holding my shoulders, framing me in his gaze.

"I'm so sorry," I said, and started crying.

We hugged. I wondered, as sobs convulsed me, if he was crying too but somehow knew he wasn't. It was my job to cry for both of us. Still, my grief was genuine, even if I didn't know exactly what it was for. Was it for Arlene, whom I'd met exactly once? ("Take care of yourself," she'd said, and, "It was nice to finally meet you.") Was it for Harvey, because he couldn't cry himself? Was it for both of us, sensing this might be the beginning of an even harder time than what we'd been through already? Or maybe the opposite. Maybe it marked the end of something.

The rest of the morning, I clung to him harder than I'd ever clung to any other human being. When it was time to go, he practically had to peel me away.

"Get out a lot," he instructed. "Don't just stay inside. Sun on your face is important."

"What's so great about the sun?"

"Nobody knows for sure. It does something to your retina. Elevates your mood."

"How long do you think you'll be gone?"

"I don't know. A few days, at least. Maybe a week."

"A week!"

The car service honked. I couldn't help notice the way he got up. He had a springy step, as if he was escaping. Well, with Ann whining along at 102 degrees, me crying hysterical tears, and the place reeking of cottage-cheese-colored puke, I couldn't really blame him.

"I'll call as soon as I get there."

You do that, I thought, looking out the window. Ann was so hot. A little furnace. As soon as the drugstore opened I would get her medicine, and then what?

He appeared, with that strange weightlessness people's movements have when viewed from above, like a bead of water on a griddle, riding its own steam, threw his bag in the trunk, and got in the back. You forgot your coat! I almost shouted, as if he could still hear me, through all the barriers that were already between us, then realized he was going to Florida. It hadn't really sunk in yet. He was trading being a little cold on his way to the airport for that feeling of stepping off the plane a few hours later, twenty pounds of clothing lighter, in bright sunshine.

· · ·

"How terrible," Iolanthe said.

"I know."

I was staring straight up into the open wine bottle, which I'd snuck out of the restaurant in the bag with all the food. Why did they always have that dent at the bottom? It took up so much room, gave you a totally false idea of how much wine was really left. Less than half a glass, it turned out. The waiters had been sympathetic, packing everything in plastic containers, making us promise to come again. Oh, sure, I'd wanted to say, but just to use the bathroom.

"I haven't talked to him. I guess he's still at the hospital, or the morgue, or wherever it is."

Io had called. I couldn't figure out why. I wasn't really paying attention. Ann had just sprayed another two tablespoons of the chalk cocktail Harvey so kindly prescribed all over my shirt. I was pissed at him for not checking in yet, even though it had only been ten hours. And now he couldn't because I was stuck on the phone with her, and there was no more wine, and I couldn't go out to buy more because I had Ann, and . . . just then a last drop of Château Whatever came out of nowhere and hit me right in the eye.

"Ow!"

"Eve, are you all right?"

"I'm doing great," I said, blinking furiously.

"You know what? You should come to my book club."

Right, I thought. Book club. Parallel Play Group for women who don't have babies yet.

"That's really nice of you, but I don't think I have the time right now."

"This is what I'm going to do: I already finished the book, so I'm going to send Mark over there with my copy. That way you don't have to buy it."

"No," I said, very decisively. "Ann's sick, you see, so I won't really be able to read anything for a while."

The truth was, I hadn't read anything since Ann was born. It was one of the great losses of motherhood. I used to read so much. I even remembered starting some long novel right before my due date, hiding my head in the sand. I was so terrified of what was about to happen that I had lain there, luxuriously turning page after page. Would I ever be able to do that again? Just waste time?

Iolanthe hadn't listened to a word I said.

"Mark should get outside anyway. He's been hammering nails all day."

In nothing but shorts, I visualized lazily. Or overalls with no shirt underneath. It was so hot in that loft. Or a shirt with no overalls. Or . . . what were those things called? Ah, yes, in nothing but a *loin cloth.*

"Wait, Iolanthe," I called into the phone. "Please don't—"

"Mark!"

I could hear her shouting in a nagging, shrewish tone, part of some ongoing battle, making him go out because he didn't want to.

"Hello? Hello? Please don't ask him to do anything."

Ann started to cry.

"Oh, sweetie." I forced concern into my voice. "If only you'd take your medicine instead of spitting it up all over Mommy. It would make you feel so much better. You don't know what's good for you, that's your problem."

"Eve?"

"Mark." I had her in my arms, the phone in the crook of my neck, wine dribbling down my cheek, and medicine drying on my chest. "Mark, *don't come.*"

"Why not?"

"Because it's not a good time."

Her crying was that weak, pathetic, sick-kid kind. Every breath sounded like her last.

"Can I talk to her?"

"Talk to who?"

"Ann."

I juggled them both and put the receiver next to her ear. She fought it, this alien piece of plastic, bumping against what she was trying to get away from, getting more and more agitated.

"What's wrong?" I heard his miniaturized voice croon. "What's wrong with little Ann?"

"Look, I can't—" She was wriggling too hard. I had to put her down. "I can't talk right now."

"What do you need?"

"Don't come, Mark. The place is a mess."

"I could buy ice cream."

The question was, should I try giving her more medicine, since she rejected the last dropperful? But how much more? After all, some must have gone down. I didn't want to overdose her. Or should I just wait another three hours? I looked down at my chest and tried calculating. Was that one spoonful or more like two, staining my shirt? There was also some other, chunkier piece of dried-out gook there I didn't even want to consider.

"I really can't talk now, Mark. I have to go."

"Where's Harvey?"

"He's in Florida. His mother—"

"Florida? You mean you're there by yourself? With a sick kid?"

"Io will explain. Listen—"

"You love ice cream."

He made it sound like an accusation.

"We eat frozen yogurt now," I said. "It's better for you."

"Frozen yogurt?"

"After a while you can't even tell the difference."

"You used to eat Coffee Heath Bar Crunch, remember?"

I remembered. Mining the flat pieces of Heath Bar, that hard toffee bonding with the enamel of your teeth so you'd be sucking at it for hours after. How the coffee flavor reached the very back of your throat, where almost nothing else did. How it trickled down without your even swallowing, hit some spot, scratched a very private itch . . .

"Eve!"

I had spaced out again, the way I always did with Mark. This time he sensed it, that fatal hesitation.

"I'll be there in fifteen minutes."

"No!"

He had already hung up.

Chapter Seven

Great. Harvey's gone less than twelve hours and you're already entertaining ex-boyfriends.

Mark is not an ex-boyfriend. He's more of a boy X-friend.

What does that mean?

It means I don't have to explain what I mean anymore.

No, this could be useful, a third me argued, trying to make peace between the other two. He could be my play husband.

What's a play husband?

I don't know. One you can have sex with?

I was fluttering around, tidying up, changing clothes, brushing my teeth, all at the same time.

"Are you feeling better?" I asked Ann. "Don't worry. Uncle Mark is coming."

This is sick, Eve, I thought. But why shouldn't I have a little fun? Did I have to veil myself from the dreaded Male Presence?

Yes, I liked Mark. He made me happy, more in anticipation than by his actually being here, but so what? I'd take that trade-off. And he was bringing ice cream. It's not that I wanted to be single again. Far from it. He was right. Being married gave seeing each other an entirely new significance. Everything was charged. For example, if we kissed (the notion, appearing suddenly and uninvited, was more powerful, more sensual, than the act itself had ever been) it would be full of danger, lighting up the walls of a dark and unknown cavern we found ourselves standing at the entrance to.

"Calm down," I said sternly, splashing my face, examining the remnant of my former self in the smudged mirror. What was going on? Everything was moving in different directions. My feet were on ice floes that were drifting apart. My legs were straining, doing a split.

Of course he didn't come in fifteen minutes like he'd said. He came in an hour, by which time whatever enthusiasm I had was wilted to peevish resentment. Ann was burning up. I'd tried taking her temperature, but holding her down, sticking that little baby thermometer up her butt, and then watching the clock was more than I could handle. I kept doing a gesture I remembered from my mother, feeling first her forehead, then mine, as if I could make some kind of objective comparison that way. Finally, I resorted to *willing* her fever away, passing my hands over her body like a faith healer.

"Hey," he said, when I opened the door.

"Could you take her?"

I was holding her just the way I did the first few months when Harvey came home. I would hear his key and then, before he could even finish turning it, undo the lock, yank open the door, and thrust his baby at him. I couldn't tell if doing the same thing to Mark meant I was already missing Harvey or if it was just the only way I knew how to greet a man anymore: Hand him your child and start to complain.

"She's been driving me crazy. She won't stop crying. I tried giving her medicine but half of it ended up on my shirt and now I don't know if I should give her more, or wait another two hours, or call her doctor, except I can't call her doctor because the doctor, it turns out, was lying to me about—"

"Shhh."

He was saying it to her but it had the same effect on me. Her stubby little arms were pushing against his flannel shirt. A new one, I noticed. Green. But underdressed, as usual. He hadn't shaved, either. There was a light stubble on his cheeks. Or maybe it was just late in the day.

"I think I'm cooling her down. Just from being outside."

I tried remembering what it was like when he didn't shave. What it felt like.

"So it's cold out there?"

Now that he'd actually showed up, I felt awkward. What exactly was he doing here? My fantasies crashed up against the fact of his physical existence, the horror of doing something wrong, something I couldn't take back.

"Io said if she's really hot, to put her in a tub with cold water."

"Io said that? How does she know?"

"She reads books."

"About child rearing?"

"That reminds me." He reached into his shirt—another thing about Mark was he didn't use pockets, he liked storing things closer to his body—and pulled out a thick paperback. "She said to give this to you."

It was warm, probably fragrant, from having nestled against his chest. I resisted the urge to smell it.

"Thanks."

"It's for her book club."

"Right."

I looked at him there, still frosty but warming up, those light brown dreadlocks framing narrow cheeks and bright eyes. His features were so delicate, nose like a blade, mouth like a . . . mouth like a . . .

"What?" I asked, sensing a question had flown by.

"So you think we should give her that bath?"

"Sure."

I started the water, then took her back and set her on the changing table. He watched.

"I've never been up here before. It's nice."

"Thanks."

It occurred to me, with a mixture of disappointment and re-lief, that nothing was going to happen for the simple overlooked reason that I was *so unattractive*. I had been focused on Mark, on his arrival. I hadn't really imagined what the scene would look like through his eyes. But now that he was standing here in the middle of the room I realized that me dealing with my scream-ing sick baby must be the ultimate sexual turnoff, worse even than those subway ads warning about teen pregnancy (IT'S LIKE BEING GROUNDED FOR EIGHTEEN YEARS). I mean, if this didn't make his penis go soft, nothing would.

Of course, nothing much did, I remembered, cautiously un-doing the diaper. He once admitted to me, genuinely embar-rassed, how boys on his high school track team used to call him Prod. He was so innocent he hadn't even figured out what that meant until years later.

"Are you a member of the book club too?"

"No, it's only for—"

"Only for women."

"I guess."

"So what do you do when they meet?"

He shrugged. He'd never thought about it.

I carried her past him, holding her away from my body in case she peed. He fell in behind me and we all trooped to the bathroom. The phone rang.

"Let the machine get it."

"No. You go ahead. I'll take her."

"You have to hold them."

"Don't worry about it, Eve."

"She drowns if you don't—"

"I can handle it," he said. "Get the phone."

It was hard to let go. It hadn't been, before, when he just wanted to see what she felt like. But this time she was naked and helpless. Before even saying hello, I stretched the wire far enough so, by tilting forward on one foot, I could peek around the corner into the bathroom.

It was Harvey.

"Hi," I said.

Mark was carefully lowering her with both hands. There wasn't much water. It didn't go above her belly button.

"I just got in," he began. "I meant to call you earlier but I went right to the hospital. That took forever. And then, when I got back here, no one could let me into the unit."

"The unit? You mean the apartment? What about your mother?"

"I haven't even seen her yet. I got involved in this nightmare bureaucratic runaround. First they told me to—"

"Could you just wait a minute?" I jammed the receiver against my side and hissed, "What are you doing?"

Mark looked surprised. "She said to splash water on her head. It helps bring down the fever."

"Since when is your wife such an expert on sick babies?"

"She's studying to be a therapist."

"I know. I thought you said she was a dancer."

"That's what she *is*." He frowned. Apparently I'd insulted her. "Therapy is what she's going to *do*."

"Eve?"

I could feel Harvey as a vibration, a disturbance, just under my rib cage.

"What's going on?" he asked. "Is someone there?"

"No. I mean, yes, but no one you know. Just a friend."

"How's Ann? Is everything OK? Who's there with you?"

"A girlfriend," I elaborated, wincing. I never thought I'd use that word, not in that way. It sounded so Parallel Play Group. "Alison."

"Alison?"

"She's from the playground. Ann is fine. We're giving her a bath to bring down the fever. Is it OK to pour cold water on her head?"

"It's not only OK, it's recommended."

"Well, don't sound so surprised. I know how to take care of a sick baby."

"Of course you do."

There was a silence. We both let that mutually-agreed-upon lie dissipate into the air.

"I'm glad you've got someone there with you," he tried going on, casually.

Then he choked up.

I could hear it, across all the wires and miles. I wanted to be there with him so badly, picturing him alone, surrounded by the suddenly dead possessions of someone he had loved. I retreated down the hall, uneasy leaving Mark with Ann but not wanting to betray Harvey anymore than I already had.

She had been moved, her body, twice, and whenever he got to each place it was too late. By the time he tracked her down to the third sub-basement of the hospital, it was closed for the day. He had to go back the next morning. Then there was the problem of getting into her apartment. I listened numbly, letting him talk, nodding nods he couldn't see, huddling on the futon, hugging myself against dark and cold, against the winter night, which no amount of light or heat could chase away. It was our first time apart.

"The worst thing is, I feel nothing."

"Of course you don't. It's too soon. You're in shock."

"You felt," he pointed out. "You cried."

"I cry all the time. It's like I have a leak."

"No, you don't. You don't have a leak. You're built perfectly."

"Built," I smiled. "I'm not *built* at all."

"You are," he insisted. "You're perfectly constructed."

"Have you been drinking?"

"No. Maybe I should be. Is that what you're supposed to do in situations like this? I wouldn't know." I could hear him look around. "There's probably nothing. Maybe some wine."

"I wasn't serious."

"I'm going to take her out," Mark called. "OK?"

"Shhh!"

"I'll let you get back to your friend."

"Don't be silly."

"No. I'm beat. I'll call you tomorrow."

"Are you sure?"

After he hung up, I sat there, wanting to put space between

these two parts of my life. But Mark came in, looking for me, holding Ann wrapped in a white towel. He was very proud.

"I think it worked. Feel her forehead."

She was cooler—and quieter too. We got her powdered and dressed. Then it was time for her medicine again. With Mark holding her, I managed to coax it all down. Soon, she was asleep.

"Good work."

"Everything all right?" He nodded to the phone.

"That was Harvey."

"What's going on?"

I didn't want to discuss it. I didn't want to contaminate what I just had on the phone with him, more a moment of true connection than anything we'd managed to achieve in the flesh lately, by talking about it with anyone, especially Mark.

"How about that ice cream now?"

"I think I'm tired, actually." I tried looking at him. Directly at him. I had to do this head on. "I really appreciate your coming. You were— I don't know what I would have done if you hadn't come."

"You would have been fine."

"But I think now I have to go to sleep."

I yawned, right in his face, a friendly stretching yawn, trying to say, This has all been a dream. We, you and me, us. It was nothing but a dream.

He reached out and lifted some of my hair. "What's this?"

"I know. I look like shit."

"You don't look like shit. But your hair's too long."

I wanted to take his hand away but that would be more intimate, somehow, than letting him explore just how ragged I'd allowed myself to get.

"Let me give you a cut."

"No, Mark. I told you. I have to go to bed."

"It's only nine-thirty."

"She'll be up again at five."

He found a stool in the kitchen and carried it into the bathroom.

"Mark?"

"I'm going to shampoo your hair. Then I'm going to cut it. Just a trim. It'll take twenty minutes, tops."

Maybe this is the way to sanity, I reasoned. Get your head looking organized externally, and then the brain, sensing the change, follows suit and trims its wild thoughts, gets rid of all those mental split ends that lead it down wrong paths, so you don't find yourself in two places at once anymore.

"Besides," he said, sitting me down, "I want to talk. We never get to talk."

Well, whose fault is that? I asked silently, letting his hands push me back until my neck hit the side of the sink. The sound of water started, close to my ears, and the feel of it, warm first, then steaming. He found shampoo, squirted it on, much too much, the way I remembered their doing it the one time I'd ever been to a semi-fancy salon. I had been scandalized by the waste, even though I was paying.

His fingers began working it in, not frantically scratching, the way I did in the shower, more of a kneading motion.

"Have you done this before?" My eyes were closed.

"Sure."

"To Io?"

"No."

"To who, then?"

"To myself."

"Well, that's not the same, is it?"

"Sure it is."

His thumbs reached my ears. They went right up to the base of each, making strong whorls, cleansing, loosening some invisible buildup. I felt my body sag. It was only the thick, insistent porcelain of the sink, bouncing against the back of my neck, that kept me from sliding to the floor.

"Does this hurt?"

"No. It's not like a shampoo, though. It's more of a massage."

"I'm trying to get out the tension."

"So what"—I felt my words slowing down—"do you want to talk about?"

"Nothing in particular. Lean back more." He started to rinse. "You have conditioner?"

I risked opening my eyes. The ceiling had strange shadowy shapes to it. I was so horizontal it looked like another wall, a secret one, with no windows or door. A wall you never saw but was right there, all the time.

"Why did Io send you here tonight?"

"Because she thought you needed help. Because she's a decent person." He said it like we weren't. "I told her about us."

"Yes, I know. So she trusts you. That's nice."

The conditioner slid in. I let his fingers go wherever they wanted, down farther, to the beginnings of my shoulders, to the back of my jaw. Or maybe I was making unconscious attempts to meet them. It was hard to tell. The boundaries between us blurred.

"You missed your calling," I murmured.

"She can't have kids."

"Io?"

"Her tubes are scarred. She had some sickness as a child.

They're not sure what. It screwed everything up inside. That's why she's so into physical fitness."

"Are you sure? There's all kinds of techniques for getting pregnant now. Procedures that—"

"We might adopt. I don't know."

He rinsed me again, then did that towel thing, squeezing out the water so my hair was perfectly damp, not dry or dripping. He sat me up and draped another towel around me like a cape.

"You're so good at this."

"These are lousy scissors."

He was combing carefully, a part right down the middle. I blinked once and caught him with an unusually serious expression.

"Eyes closed."

I smiled into his body heat, his warmth.

"I'm glad we can be like this."

"Be like what?"

"Talking. Not—"

"So is she mine or his?"

He raised one section of hair, the one he had touched to begin with, that had offended his sense of proportion, and snipped it off.

"What?"

"Ann."

I could hear each strand being sliced, they were so close to my ear. They sounded like the cables of a bridge being cut, one at a time. *Ping, ping, ping.* The sounds translated into shivers.

"Is she mine? Or is she his?"

"She's mine," I answered automatically. "What are you talking about?"

"You can't blame me for wondering."

I opened my eyes but there was a distorted side of hand blotting everything out. He had a hunk of hair, half my head, he was tugging at with a comb, trimming off the edges. His smell, that familiar combination of beeswax, pot, and . . . just him, his musky take-a-bath-once-a-week self, was beginning to overpower the floral scent of the conditioner, which I now for some reason remembered was called Summer Evening. How ridiculous was that, naming a scent after a time of day?

"Well?" he asked.

"Are you serious?"

My mind was running along any possible random outskirt of thought to avoid dealing with this totally unacceptable turn the conversation had taken.

"Ever since we met that time in the park, I'd been hoping you'd tell me. I didn't want to—" He stopped. "I wanted to be cool about it. But I can't, anymore. I have to know."

"Have to know what?"

"Is she my child?"

I was really afraid he was making me into a bald person. The scissors were clacking away. But there was nothing I could do. I was trapped by this maniac who towered over me, blocking the light.

"We broke up"—my palms clenched and unclenched—"about a year before I even met Harvey. You said you couldn't handle it. You said I was *too intense,* remember?"

He didn't have to remember. I remembered. I had bronzed the words. No, they were fragments of bullet, lodged in my heart. Whenever I moved a certain way they ached, so I learned to move in a totally different way, a new walk, except it wasn't really a walk, it was more a permanent limp.

"I'm talking about after," he said.

"After was nothing. After was me calling and you hanging up."

And after that was far worse; I allowed myself to truly remember. After was as degrading and humbling a time as I had ever spent in my life. Even when I stopped hounding and pestering him, I couldn't stop stroking objects he had given me, or freezing suddenly in the middle of the street at a sound or touch or feeling that was some leftover bit of love memory I hadn't dealt with, that I hadn't formally sobbed over those evenings, those long, hopelessly alone evenings. All that, I had managed to cover over with a thick growth of scar tissue, change into a nostalgic numbness, an emotional amnesia. And now he was threatening to bring it all back to life again with this—it struck me with the force of a revelation—crazy idea.

Wait a minute.

He was crazy, not me!

"Mark." I almost laughed, able to breathe again. "Do you actually think—?"

"Hold still." He was slicing right along my forehead. I could feel the cold metal against my skin. "It's not funny."

"No, it isn't," I gasped, trying to hold back this condescending joy I felt.

He really had me going there. It was such a relief to be smarter than him. It was the only card I held. But I forgot about it so often, willfully denied it, as if intelligence was the opposite of sex. Why? Why set the two in opposition?

"We weren't seeing each other then, Mark," I said gently. "Just because you're thinking about someone, just because you had this . . . intense relationship with them, doesn't mean that a year later you can possibly be involved in who their kid is. I mean, that's the one part of you that *doesn't* hang around inside me. In a way, it's very romantic, what you're asking, but—"

"There was that time you showed up at the loft."

"When?" I asked, feeling just the most far-off obscure panic, like when the corner of a rug has been turned over.

"You remember. That night you came and stood under my window? Until I had to come down and get you?"

"Oh, that time." I didn't actually remember, but I accepted what he said. It sounded right. It conformed to some sketchy outlines, colored in some black-and-white incidents I had floating around in my head that I never bothered to put in any coherent order. "But we didn't do anything."

He gave a quiet laugh, a short forced-out breath, and then I remembered we had done something, but it was obviously a mistake. A relapse. We had proved to each other for the last time just how wrong this was, that's how I saw it. It didn't count.

"And that's what you're basing this whole fantasy on?"

"It's not a fantasy. It really happened."

"It was one time."

"One time is all it takes."

"It was before I even met Harvey."

"Was it?"

"Of course. You think I'd be standing under your window for hours like an idiot if I was already seeing someone else?"

"You're positive?"

"Mark, women keep track of these things."

"Even you?"

"Believe me, if there was even the possibility of my being pregnant by you, that's all I would have been aware of until—"

"Until when?"

"Until I knew I wasn't."

"And you weren't."

"No."

His comb did a long sweep. My hair felt detangled and clean. It tingled with an inner glow. He went on to the other side, digesting what I'd told him.

"I thought, because of her age . . . I don't know. It seemed right. The time line. Or close enough."

"It's not horseshoes."

"Huh?"

"Never mind. But I'm touched, I really am. I would have loved to have had your child."

"Well, that's a lie."

"Yes." I giggled.

He gripped my head in both hands, not a haircutting maneuver, pressing in. I opened my eyes. He had raised them so we were staring right into each other and, for the first time, I saw, in his, *pain,* the hurt of a person who'd had something taken away.

"You're sure, Eve?"

I nodded. Or tried to. The vise weakened. I felt the purpose go out of his fingers.

"I'm sorry," I said.

"I can still love her, right?"

"Ann? If you want to."

He stood back and looked at me, looked at my hair, the job he was doing, his handiwork, then came forward again, to finish.

"So," I couldn't help but ask, "is that the only reason you've been coming around? Because you thought she might be yours?"

"Not the only reason."

"But the main one."

"I don't think that way."

No, you just don't think, I wanted to say. Period.

I tried keeping my eyes open, glaring, while he worked. But he looked so sad.

"Io thought it would be a good idea if I reconnected with you."

"Really? Why?"

"I told you. She's a decent person. She thought it would help me work through some unfinished feelings."

"Will you leave her?"

"There." He tilted my head one last time. "Leave Io? Because she can't have kids? You must think I'm a real jerk."

"No, I don't."

For the first time ever, I had something he desired, something he couldn't have. It made me feel guilty.

"You must have thought about it, though."

"All done. Turn around."

He held on to me, which was a good thing, because in the crowded bathroom, with the stool taking up most of the floor, I almost fell. I leaned forward into the mirror to see past my face, around each side.

"Mark, it's fantastic."

He picked up the stool.

"Really," I called.

I looked sleek and flapperish. Like I didn't have a care in the world. He'd given me a little of his fairy dust, his youth, which was why he seemed older, I thought, back in the hallway. He came out of the kitchen and got ready to leave.

"Aren't you going to help me with the ice cream?"

"No. I should be going."

"Poor Mark."

I wanted to finger what I could see would one day be his graying sideburns. It was the trick—I'd never done it on him before—of seeing him middle-aged, because he'd finally met tragedy. He wasn't an untouched boy anymore.

Instead, I opened the door for him. He stopped, halfway through.

"You hurt your foot."

"When?"

"That last time. Well, right after. When you were hurrying out. Trying to get away."

"Oh, right."

"You wouldn't let me help you. You were in such a rush. You bashed your foot against the doorframe. Really hurt your toe. I wanted to take you to the hospital but you wouldn't let me. Don't you remember?"

"No."

"That was the last picture I had of you, limping down the stairs. You could hardly walk. Holding on to the banister. Not letting me help. That's why it all felt so . . . incomplete. Until now."

He hugged me, a brotherly hug, enveloped me, made me another thing he could keep close to his body, where he stored what he cared about.

"That's why I'm glad you let me help this time. Tonight."

Then he took off, without turning back. Some keys he had hanging off a belt loop jingled.

I looked down and flexed my toes. I felt for old pain. For a familiar ache. My head, with its pound less of hair, was too light on my neck. It saw differently now, at new angles. I stood there, trying to piece things together. Yes. I had hit my foot on the doorway, going out. Of course. He was right. Wearing sandals.

What I remembered most were the sandals. I still had them. I had fractured my toe, it turned out later—only a few hours later, in fact, when I noticed the pain, accepted it, walking on the street, still in a daze—and from there I went to the free clinic, and that, of course, was where I met Harvey.

I had never connected the two. Never seen them as part of a story, a story bigger than each taken separately.

So the limp Mark left me with was real. Not that there was any chance of him being Ann's biological father. That was the kind of thing you didn't lose track of, even when you were as far out in space as I had been. Of course he didn't know that. He didn't really accept it, even now, after I'd told him. He was crazy about her.

I toyed with the idea of falling back in love with Mark. No, of *escaping* love. Of returning, instead, to what I'd had before. Something less personal, something where we didn't always have the goods on each other. Marriage was so horribly intimate.

*   *   *

The next morning, she was all better. I gave her the antibiotic, bundled her into extra-warm clothes, and went for a walk. I wandered around the neighborhood, hugging her body to me through the Snugli. There was nothing I needed to do. I just wanted to stare into the sun, elevate my mood, burn back some of the insanity that was creeping in at the edges of my thought.

Mark, of course, wasn't the answer. Harvey had been there at her birth and every day since. That was far more important than flying her like an airplane or making her laugh by playing peek-a-boo. Right?

"You have *got* to develop better taste in men," I scolded her.

We walked past the playground. The benches had snow on them. You couldn't even push open the gate. I stood outside the fence, gazing at the equipment as if it were some Eden I'd been expelled from. Sun had cleared the middle of the slide. Slush was slumped at its bottom. The exposed metal shone. Water dripped from the seats of the swings.

We kept walking and left the park.

Back on Seventh Avenue, Alison was coming out of the hardware store. She had Dominic in a fancy jogging stroller, the kind that could roll right over most obstacles.

"This is really funny," I called. "I just said I was with you when I wasn't."

She looked at me with such an utter lack of recognition I thought for a moment I had made a mistake. She was wearing dark glasses.

"What are you buying that for?"

I pointed to the gardening claw she was holding, what you would use for raking through weedy soil or getting out crabgrass maybe, something very suburban and unlikely.

"It's for Dominic."

"You let him play with that? Isn't it a little sharp?"

"Dominic my husband."

The door to the hardware store opened again and she gave a quick look behind before starting to walk. I tried staying next to her even though it was hard, because the jogging stroller was extra-wide and there were piles of snow lining the street.

"Slow down, will you?"

"I don't like the salesmen at that place."

"Why not?"

"They kept watching me."

I noticed how she slipped the claw into her coat pocket and that it hadn't come in a bag or with a receipt.

"Did you take that, Alison?"

"Of course not."

"Yes, you did. You shoplifted it. That is such an amazing coincidence, because I just took a piece of fabric from—"

"Oh, you're from Janice's play group, aren't you?"

I couldn't understand why she was acting like she didn't remember me, why she was being so stiff and formal. Had she forgotten? I involuntarily licked my lips, trying to retrieve some of the taste or sensation from the time—

"I haven't been back lately. We've been very busy. Dominic and I went to the museum yesterday, didn't we?"

"That must have been exciting."

"Putting them in front of art stimulates their mental development."

I looked down. It wasn't his mental development I would be worried about. He was one of those steroid babies, really plumped out, like a turkey. We came to an icy patch. She slipped. I reached out to grab her, but she held on to the stroller handle instead, using it as a walker to keep herself up. That's when I noticed she was wearing high heels. And stockings.

"Alison?"

"What's your daughter's name again?"

"Ann."

"How are you, Ann?"

Fine! I was tempted to pipe back, like a bad ventriloquist.

"We were just getting supplies for our garden."

"You have a garden? I thought you lived in an apartment."

"It's going to be an inside garden, isn't it, Dominic? With flowers made of tissue paper. And maybe even a lake. With fishies."

She stopped to come around and adjust his hat, keeping her legs together, bending them sideways. She tickled him under the chin and talked baby talk to him. She had gone back to being the first Alison we had met, that day at the Parallel Play Group, but even more proper and fake. It was an act, a way over-the-top Upper East Side mom act, much crazier than when I'd seen her being crazy. The woman who had dragged me out to Snoopy's, with whom I'd listened to that overheard conversation, was nowhere to be seen.

"We have to go," she said. "Don't we? We need our rest."

"I thought maybe we could get a cup of coffee and let the kids play again. I had this really weird experience I wanted to tell you about, with a phone call, just like the time we—"

"Ugh. I hate how unsanitary it is at Osbourne's. Do you think they ever wash those toys?"

"Probably not."

She got back up and smoothed her coat. She was smiling, this glazed, reflecting smile, not showing anything.

"Wait." I didn't want her to go but couldn't think of anything to make her stay. I said the first thought that came into my head. "What's the name of that woman? The one you were dumping Dominic with before?"

"I never *dumped* Dominic anywhere."

"You said she was older and she took care of kids."

She pretended not to remember.

"That time we met at the Laundromat and came back to my place. The time we—"

"Oh. You mean Frances. That was an emergency." She looked both ways, as if we were under surveillance. "I'm not sure I could really recommend her."

"She doesn't wash her toys?"

"Her house is just a little seedy. You know what I mean? And she takes in so many children. They don't get much individualized attention, which is very important at this age, don't you think?"

I could see myself in her glasses. I liked my haircut. I really wanted to talk to her, even if she was acting nutty. She made me happy. She was this potential antidote to loneliness. But when I tried to express even a little of that, it came out in my usual free-form chatter, which didn't help.

"This is so weird, because I lied. Last night I told Harvey I had run into you, when I hadn't. But now I have, so that kind of makes it all right. Although," I went on, more to myself, "I said you were from the playground, which still isn't true. Yet. Maybe we could sit there now, if you don't like Osbourne's. We could brush the snow off the benches and—"

"We have to go," she said brightly. "It was nice seeing you."

"What's Frances's address?"

She made this big show of not remembering. She even tapped her head.

"Let me see. Fifth Street off Sixth Avenue? Near the corner? I'm not sure."

"Is everything OK? You seem kind of nervous."

"Everything's great." She was either smiling or baring her teeth at me. "But we have to fly now. We're on a very tight schedule. Dominic, say goodbye."

"Goodbye, Dominic."

I watched them leave. I told Harvey I had seen her when I hadn't. But now I had. The future was just as jumbled up as the past. Lying was the key. Lying to myself and to others. Maybe lies weren't as bad as everyone said. Maybe they were really tapping into some Universal Vision where you saw what was going to happen before it did. Because how important was the order in which things occurred?

I felt the ground giving way under my feet.

"Mommy's tired," I explained to Ann, still staring after them. "Mommy needs a little break."

. . .

You could see babies through the ground-floor window. Hundreds of them, I imagined, from the outside, peering while I waited for someone to answer the buzzer. But when I got in, it was more like ten or twelve, some sleeping in strollers, others crawling around. A few bigger kids were camped out in front of a TV. More than the Department of Child Services would have allowed, I figured, but then again she was only charging eight dollars an hour. Frances was an energetic woman with white hair. She seemed totally unfazed by the chaos going on all around her. Her mother sat in the corner. She made it sound like the old lady helped, but I didn't see how. She was so shrunken she seemed more like one of the kids. Then I saw she had an infant in her lap.

"And this is my daughter," she completed introducing me to the staff, as a grumpy, middle-aged woman came out of the kitchen and stomped past us with a bottle.

It wasn't at all what I imagined a day-care center or a preschool would be like. It was just a house, a floor-through apartment, with about seven times as many kids as it was designed to hold. But there was something very friendly and warm about it.

"How long have you been doing this?"

"Oh, years," she said vaguely. "I always took in babies. A lot of women around here did, once their own left. It used to just be part of things."

Two of them began to cry.

"I'll be right back."

She waded in and picked them both up.

"What's the matter with you two?" she squawked, looking from one to the other. "Are you fighting again?"

All right, this is definitely the gateway to being officially designated a Bad Mother, I thought. Then I looked around and asked, Are all the women who left their kids here bad mothers? And what about Frances and her mother and her daughter? Three generations. Are they all bad mothers too? It seemed like it was just a concept used to keep you in line, like Original Sin. No matter how hard you tried, how could you not be bad? After all, if you hadn't been "bad" you wouldn't be a mother to begin with. We were all of us just trying to get through the day.

I lifted Ann out of the Snugli and put her on the floor. She crawled over to investigate colored rings stacked on a soft rounded spike, and started gnawing away at the plastic. She seemed happy enough. Still . . .

"I don't know," I said dubiously. "I just have to do something for a few hours."

"Go," she said. "She'll be fine. All young mothers need some time."

"Should I say goodbye?"

"It's better if you don't."

I walked out and got as far as the steps leading up to the sidewalk when a scream came through the window. I turned and looked inside again, but it was someone else's kid, wailing inconsolably while the daughter tried to give it a bottle. Ann was just where I'd left her, playing. Then I realized that eventually she *would* cry, in the natural course of things, and I better not be standing here when she did. Besides, I was paying for this time. I couldn't afford to waste it.

Now, what did I truly want?

"To be alone," I answered aloud. "To be home, by myself, alone."

I went up the rest of the steps, walked home as fast as I could, and shut the door. I turned each lock, picturing the metal bolts sliding across, barring the entrance. I fixed the chain to its holder. If I'd had a chair that propped under the knob, I might have done that too.

Now what? I prompted.

Before, I never had free time. Not like this. Not with such pressure to make the most of it. I got out the journal, flipped past the pages I had scratched up or sketched on, and very neatly wrote:

Dear

Dear who?

I decided to leave that blank. I could fill in whom the letter was going to later, after I saw what it said.

Dear _____,

I stared at the pencil. This made no sense. How could I write a letter when I didn't know whom it was addressed to? An overwhelming exhaustion came over me. I went to bed, cried a little, and slept.

I dreamed I was back at the Colony. I was my mother now, taking care of me. Nothing happened in the dream. It wasn't a story. We were both in each other's arms. It was winter outside. I held her to me and watched the ice form on the inside of the window. It detached itself in chunks that I could slide around. But I pressed too hard and things broke, the glass or the ice, I couldn't tell which. Cold air rushed in. There was a pink tinge to everything. I had ruined the laundry again, mixed colors and whites. My hand was bleeding but I felt no pain. Oh, of course, I reasoned, it numbs you, the cold. But when spring comes, then you're going to feel it. I looked around on the floor for the broken piece, to plug the hole, and Mark bent over first to get it. He was so good at finding things. "But what are you doing here?" I asked. "Harvey's in Florida," he said, which was news to me. And then I thought, Yes, of course, he's in Florida, and for some reason that made everything all right, gave me a freedom I didn't have before. I pulled my dress down over me, because I had been naked this whole time, and admired myself in the mirror. My reflection was almost ready. It would just take a little more time. It was one of those slow mirrors, but the reflection it did show, when it finally came, would be better than a regular one. Deeper. I waited patiently. And opened my eyes.

It was dark. Dark in the bedroom. My body jerked to sitting, sweating and disoriented. I didn't know where I was and, worse, didn't want to know, was afraid of finding out. I had drifted far from myself. One thought came to me: Ann. Where was Ann? And then, Oh my God, what time is it? followed by the whole trailing interconnected rest of them, fitting together and weighing me down. I reached for the clock. I had slept on one of my arms, turning it into dead weight, and had to heave it forward with my torso. It flopped on the night table, cold and ineffective, a flipper. Blood burned as it entered the pinched-off veins. I squinted at the hands, trying to make sense of their position: 1:05. They were on top of each other, that's what had confused me: 1:05 in the morning? I looked to the window and saw the shade was down, that it was day, not night. One in the afternoon. I had only been asleep for an hour.

I got up, rubbing my eyes. The tailor's dummy was still in the corner. Bits of my dream, shiny flecks, twinkled just beyond my ability to understand. I was the me of several years ago, waking up alone, not caring what time of day it was because nobody knew about me, nobody was waiting. I did what I always did then, hauled out my sewing machine. There was something reassuring about how heavy it was. It was an old-fashioned monster, packed with steel, so much more of a load than its small size made you think. I set it up and plugged it in. I couldn't remember when I'd last used it. There hadn't been some grand ceremony when I put it away, retiring it. It had been so unconscious, the change in my life. So unthinking. I never said, I'm giving up work for motherhood. How could I? I didn't know what those words meant. I found the fabric from the store. When I'd gotten back, the day of our anniversary, Harvey was already waiting for me, ready to whisk me off to our surprise dinner. I'd been so flustered I jammed the material I'd stolen high on the closet shelf, under some extra sheets. Now I unfolded it on the floor and took a look for the first time at what I'd taken.

I was disappointed. It wasn't for making clothes. It was a very gauzy, almost weblike rayon, fraying at the edges. You could see it coming apart. On the other hand, it was beautiful, in a showy knock-your-eyes-out way, iridescent green with raised black polka dots that were furry, part of an endless butterfly wing. I had no idea what it was intended for. Not everyday use, that was certain. It was too delicate. For decoration, then. But decoration of what? The light caught it and shifted its spectrum.

I'd taken a lot more than I thought. It kept unfolding until it covered the floor, three yards at least. Enough for a dress. Not a dress you could wear, but . . .

I got out my tools: my ruler, pins, and fabric shears. This wasn't how you did it. You were supposed to have a pattern. And I did, but not one I knew. The pattern would come after the fact, I decided, getting down on my hands and knees. I didn't have much time, either. I was aware, every second she was away, that I had left Ann. The anxiety that she might be missing me sharpened my senses, gave my movements an urgency, as if this was somehow a way of getting back to her. One wrong cut, I reminded myself, and it's ruined. But I had made hundreds of dresses. On some obscure intuitive level, I knew what I was doing.

I was still copying, just not from a source. It was the same process as when I used to have a photo and my own sketches to refer to, with cutout pieces of tissue paper or, when it was really complicated and I didn't want to screw up, a mock-up first in white muslin. You had to see it as panels, then go from flat to round. That was the hardest thing to do in your mind. And you had to hold it all together, what didn't exist yet, willing it to be, because as soon as you stopped, it stopped too. It froze and ceased, not having any momentum of its own. So I had to keep going, the dots swimming before my eyes, the green shimmering to blue, to yellow. Something was guiding my hand, I couldn't imagine what. Some long-repressed memory fighting its way to the surface. I had done this before. That was the overwhelming sense I had. I was making the ultimate copy. But from what original?

The phone was ringing. I let it go. Harvey's voice came on and gave me a number to call him back at.

The material was maddening to work with. I could see it was going to be impossible to sew together. This whole thing was a dumb idea, doomed to failure. But I couldn't stop. I crawled and cut and crawled some more. How long had it been since I tasted pins? They slid in my mouth. I felt again the bizarre fear I always had of swallowing one. Each piece I draped carefully on the dummy, trying not to damage the fabric, fitting them together, noting with pleasure how the sections met—overlapped a bit, yes, but that was good. Room for error. Wiggle room.

When they were all pinned, I stood back and saw that, while it wasn't some fabulous creation, it was a dress. Or the beginning of one. Of course it was a miracle that with no pattern and measurements, with a length of stolen fabric and an hour's feverish concentration, I had made even that.

I circled it, checking to see that all the raw pieces hung together. It was floor-length, not fancy though, not a ballroom gown. More like a pioneer dress, but without the puffy sleeves. Where had I seen it before? It was simple. I liked its simplicity, although the fabric, being wild and not for use, gave the whole thing a strange science-fiction quality. And then I saw, not in some power-packed tidal wave of recall that unlocked everything all at once but quietly, with surprise and regret, that this wasn't anything new at all; it was the first dress I had ever worn and the only dress I had worn for many years, what all the girls and women during my childhood wore. It was a Colony dress, the uniform of my youth. My mother had made ours with a needle and thread, by the light of a kerosene lamp, in heavy cotton:

navy or black, white for special occasions. No ornamentation, no ostentation, permitted.

I went up and fingered the sheer gauze, half expecting its powdery colors to come off on my hand. A line had definitely been crossed, though into what I couldn't say.

Chapter Eight

. . . which still doesn't explain how I found myself listening to Martin Cooper's sex confessions through the half-open door of his hotel bathroom.

"He called it a monk's room. I was disappointed he did not come up with *cell*, a monk's *cell*, but plowed on with the obvious rejoinder of his crediting me with more restraint than I possessed."

"Are you all right in there?"

Steam was pouring out. He must have had the shower on pure HOT.

"It all fell on deaf ears, buried perhaps too deep in the baroque intricacies of his curls. There I go lying again. In fact, his hair was long and straight, with a little flip at the end like a ski jump."

"You know, I could come back later."

"We met at a bar called Tooled Leather, which I found amusing but he did not, before proceeding to what they have the temerity to call a McDonald's *restaurant,* where our prejudices were reversed. We then returned here and, after a brief financial negotiation, waited for me to travel the few remaining inches that lay between us. Alas, the evening—I cannot be more specific—had succeeded in paralyzing the one normally aggressive bone in my body."

"I really don't want to hear about—"

"Being impotent is like reaching for and not finding your wallet. There follows a wild-eyed eternity of self-recrimination and painful acceptance—my passport, credit cards, the picture of Mother—all of which takes ten minutes. The night was still young, even if I, apparently, was not. Even if my manhood was counterfeiting an overboiled length of tagliatelle."

"That's it. I'm out of here. There's something I want to leave you with, though."

The water stopped.

"Then I did a very foolish thing indeed. I dialed room service for a bottle of your famous Kentucky bourbon whiskey, which explains the lamentable state you find me in this morning."

He came out wearing a terry-cloth robe, the kind with a belt knotted at the side. Maybe it was because he had just used the word, but a monk was exactly what it made him look like, short and plump. Pink-faced.

"Sit."

The room was bare. I saw what his visitor from last night meant. All the pictures had been taken down and turned to the wall. There was only one chair, and it was piled high with dirty laundry. I sat on the edge of the bed, clutching the plastic bag to my chest. He scooped up the clothes, went over to the corner, let them fall, then came back and sat across from me, putting his feet on the mattress. They made a dip my body slid down into.

"Where is your child?"

"With a lady in the neighborhood who takes care of kids. Did you still have to pay him?" I wanted to show I'd been listening. "The guy you said you couldn't . . . you know."

"Oh, yes. He was quite apologetic. Took it personally, he did. Which was a mistake, of course." He yawned, stretching his arms. "Nothing personal about it. How did you find me? If you'll pardon my asking."

"You said you were staying here. I listened, that day I helped you make that girl cry. You said you were staying at the Gramercy Park Hotel."

"Well, paying attention to what I say certainly puts you in a distinct minority. However, I still don't see why—"

"I brought you something."

None of this was going as planned. Originally, I was going to leave it at the desk, with a note. But when I asked for his room number they sent me right on up. They must have thought I was a member of the crew.

"Ah, yes. I must say, ever since you came in I have been eyeing that package of yours with quite a bit of trepidation."

"Oh, that's just the bag I used. It's not really from the Berkeley Meat Emporium."

"Good."

Even when I had got to the door, I thought I would just knock, be met by someone else, thrust my ridiculous offering into unwilling hands, and scurry off, hoping it would eventually get to him.

"It shouldn't even be folded," I stalled. "It should be on a hanger. But I didn't have any of that dry-cleaning plastic to put over it and I was afraid of getting splashed. Besides, it's a little embarrassing to go around with a—"

"If you do not remove that cartoon rendering of a soon-to-be-eviscerated cow from my vision, I am going to be sick."

I took out the dress. It had taken me the rest of the week to finish, after the initial frenzy of realizing what I wanted to do wore off. I had figured out a way of making the material stay together by a series of strips lining the seams on either side, just enough to hold the fabric in place without sacrificing its sheer shimmering quality. But here in the curtained light, the material lost some of its sparkle. He made no move to take it. I laid it carefully on the floor in front of us.

"It's a dress."

Was it such a bizarre, formless, asymmetrical puddle of material that he couldn't even tell? My worst fears were coming true. Maybe all the magic and specialness it held only existed in my own head.

"I mean, not a dress a real person could wear, of course. It's completely unwearable. But an idea for a dress."

I waited for him to say something and, when he didn't, stumbled on.

"I thought, maybe you might have an opening for someone who could make costumes. I wanted to show you what I could do. That way, if you ever needed . . ."

Saying the words out loud, trying to launch my fantasies in the dead air of the hotel room, made it clear just how pathetic and unrealistic they were. I waited for him to tell me that, but he didn't. He stared past everything, down into the colors.

"You are too late."

"What do you mean?"

"We are almost done here. We have only a few more scenes to shoot. Then we leave."

"Oh."

He got up and walked around without touching it, tracing the curve of an invisible circle.

"You made this?"

"Not really. I can't make things. I can only copy."

"Copying is making. In the act of copying you inevitably add something of your own. You fail to copy exactly, and in that failure are sown the seeds of your originality."

"I wouldn't know about that."

He shook his head, annoyed.

"What, precisely, is your problem?"

"Problem? I don't have a problem."

"That is hardly fair. I just told you my problem. The least you can do is reciprocate."

"When did you tell me your problem?"

"Just now. When I spoke of the previous evening."

"Because you couldn't—?"

"I fear I am losing my powers, becoming a shadow of my former self. I fear some lifelong flame, some pilot light inside me, has been snuffed out. That is my problem. And now you, a woman who, for all I know, has been following me for months, if not years, force yourself into my hotel room—"

"They said I should go on up!"

"—at the crack of dawn, flings a disturbing fashion statement on the floor, and claims, by contrast, to be a shining example of mental health. To be in no distress at all. Is that truly the case? I think not. I think there is something on *your* mind, as well. Otherwise, what are you doing here?"

"I told you, I hoped you might have a job for me."

He began to turn away, giving up.

"I think"—the words rushed out before I could stop them— "I may have made a mistake."

"A mistake concerning what?"

"Parenthood, marriage, my whole life."

I was about to cry. He pretended not to notice. Instead, he reached out and lifted the shoulder of the dress, very carefully, as if it might bite. Watching him comfort the wrong thing, what I'd made, not me, got me even more upset.

"Is there any of that whiskey left?"

"At ten o'clock in the morning?"

"It's either that or I'm going to ask you to hold me."

"On the windowsill, behind the drapes."

I went over and looked out. There was just another building and, if you looked higher, a water tower.

"Pardon my asking, but isn't the person to whom you should be subjecting this confession the child's father?"

"It's none of his business."

"Really!"

"Oh, who's to say men actually have anything to do with making babies?" I snapped. "They certainly don't act like it, after. Is there a glass anywhere?"

"By the sink, I believe."

"Never mind." I took a sip from the bottle.

"What do you mean men don't have anything to do with making babies?"

"Well, that whole sperm-egg-pregnancy thing is pretty self-important, don't you think? It could just be another myth designed to inflate their egos, trying to make them seem indispensable when really they're the opposite."

"I thought it was generally agreed upon that—"

"That's what you've been *taught*." Suddenly I was very excited. "And, sure, it makes sense on the surface, but that's because all the evidence is arranged to make it look scientific. If you go back a hundred years, I bet you'll find all kinds of universally accepted 'facts' about the world that turn out to be total fairy tales dreamed up by women-hating professors with beards and cigars."

I drank some more. I forgot how good it was. Why did people always say whiskey tasted bad? And it made me so smart.

"Maybe," I went on, "it has something to do with when you're around a man but isn't directly connected to him. Have you ever thought of that?"

"So you are saying pregnancy may be an allergic reaction?"

"Yes! A defense mechanism, designed to drive him away. You get fat and cranky and he stops *bothering* you, ideally."

"I can see the world of biology lost a great talent when you opted to become a—" He stopped. "What exactly *are* you?"

"Me? I'm nothing."

The simple truth of it hit me. I was nothing. All those words, girl, wife, mother, were not real things to be at all. My self-worth was in free fall. The liquor went down without hitting bottom. I was a pipe, a conduit, leading from nowhere to nowhere.

He didn't stop me. That wasn't his style. He was focused back on the dress.

"I like this very much. Why 'unwearable,' though?"

"What?"

"You said it was unwearable. Why?"

"Because of the material. It's for decoration. If you tried doing anything, it would tear." I laughed. "It's so typical. I spent all this time making a thing I couldn't even use."

"Not you, perhaps, but I can see someone else in it."

"Who?"

"Jennifer. The young woman you were so accommodating to the other day. Are you willing to sell it to me?"

"You can have it." I had gone from hopelessness to euphoria to hopelessness again in about seven seconds. "I should go. I have to pick up my daughter. My husband's coming back from Florida tonight. I'm trying to make pot roast for dinner."

"Three potentially nauseating prospects," he agreed. "But don't you hear what I am saying? I can use this dress in my film. It can be what she wears when she finally encounters—"

"Excuse me, but I don't *care* what happens in your movie."

He smiled. "Of course you don't. Why should you?"

I immediately got apologetic. "I've been acting like an idiot. I have to go."

He came over and took the bottle away. Our fingers intertwined. His hand was so small it slipped into mine.

"Not just yet."

I found I couldn't move. "So you're almost done here? You're leaving?"

"I am afraid so."

"Where to?"

"Morocco."

"Morocco!"

"I had to move heaven and earth to justify the expense. As an alternative, my producers kept proposing a sandbox, basically, with a large lightbulb that was supposed to mimic the desert sun. I told them. . . ."

A monk. I wanted to tug at his robe, the big floppy knot that was just made to slide apart. I wanted the sides to fall open and show I had provoked this miracle resurrection. He felt it too, what was going on. I could tell, because for the first time he stumbled in his talk, left a sentence hanging.

We sat a minute, on the bed. I could feel his hard blue gaze. He was interested in what I was making him feel. Intrigued.

"I grew up in a cult, a magical society," I heard myself say. "And even though I turned my back on it, years ago, it's left me . . . living in a world of signs. Everything seems like a clue. Or a warning."

"Which am I?"

"You're someone to follow, someone to give my soul over to and let deal with the pesky question of what comes next."

"Am I really?"

"But you're the last. I can't really do that anymore. There are other people involved now. Besides, you're going away."

"Is that what you came for?" He gently disengaged his fingers. "To wish me a pleasant journey?"

I shook my head. "I just came here to give you the dress."

The phone rang.

"The dress we used to wear."

While he answered, I looked around. The room seemed smaller and more cluttered.

"That was my assistant," he announced, hanging up.

"The guy with the clipboard?"

"Jonathon. He is on his way up."

A chill came over me. "Will he think I spent the night?"

"Would it bother you if he did?"

"Maybe," I said.

"Why should it, though? What awaits you at home? A squalling child? A clueless husband? The inept preparation of a rustic beef dish?" He let his robe slip to the floor and went off to the bathroom again. The water started, in the sink, this time.

"No, stay here a little longer. I insist. The look on poor Jonathon's face when he opens the door will be worth the price of admission, I assure you."

I tested my legs. Very carefully, as if they might break, I pushed on the bed until my feet touched the floor.

"I enjoy talking to you. People don't approach me anymore. Certainly not with the degree of naked honesty you've exhibited. That's a large part of my problem, I suppose. The isolation from fellow feeling. From genuine intimacy."

I eased off the mattress and crossed the room.

"As I finally said to Albert, my young Texan friend from last night, 'It's lonely on the top.' He, of course, misunderstood. That hair of his, no doubt. All those cascading curls."

This is where I came in, I realized, turning the doorknob.

"He tried to correct me. 'You mean lonely *at* the top,' he said. I didn't have the heart to explain. . . ."

The hallway was a different world. So quiet and impersonal. I was wet from steam. A bell signaled the elevator door opening. Jonathon, the clipboard guy, stepped out. Before he could see me, I faced away from him and walked quickly in a different direction, down the long corridor. Toward the stairs.

* * *

I wasn't really having a nervous breakdown, I decided. It was just early and I'd drunk that bourbon on an empty stomach. Getting hysterical, flirting with a gay impotent film director in a bathrobe—none of that seemed unusual. And the morning hadn't been a complete waste. I'd invented a new drink: the Good Mother, liquor and anything. No, liquor and nothing. That was the key. Take your life straight.

"And then there's the Supermom." I tried not to breathe right onto Ann, whom I'd just picked up. "Which is even *more* liquor and nothing. The more liquor taking the place of the extra nothing. Hey, maybe I should open a bar. What do you think? Huh?"

The phone was ringing. I heard it all the way up the steps. I didn't hurry. Using my newly acquired psychic powers, I could tell it had been ringing for hours. And would go on ringing. It had settled into a nice rhythm.

"Where have you been?" a voice accused.

"Hello?"

"Have you seen them? I hear they're all over."

"Marjorie?"

"The bastard. Why didn't you call?"

"You mean the flyers? I don't have your number. Anyway, they're mostly gone now. Do you realize you've been away for almost—?"

"He wants joint custody. I am not having my children raised by some perky little Canadian."

"She's Canadian? I didn't know that. Are you home now? Can I come over?"

"You have to do something for me."

What about, Hi, how are you? I was silently asking. What about, Tell me *your* troubles, Eve?

"You have to go to my house. You still have the keys?"

"Of course I have the keys. I've been feeding your cat, remember? There's also one plant I'm worried about. It's got these white spots on the leaves. I can't tell if they're supposed to be there, or if—"

"I need you to get my financials."

"Your what?"

"There are several files. I'll tell you where to find them. I can't let them fall into the wrong hands."

"The wrong hands? Marjorie, what are you talking about? Where are you?"

She wasn't at the phone anymore. She was whispering to someone off to the side.

"Marjorie?"

"Listen, Eve."

"You know, things have been pretty crazy here since you left." I still had Ann in my arms. I hadn't even taken off my coat. I was plopped down on the futon letting her sandwich me against its lumpy filling. "For one thing, Harvey's mother—"

"Can you do this for me right now?"

"Go to your house, you mean? Couldn't I do it later? I'm going to make brisket, which is really pot roast. Did you know that? The guy at the meat store, the butcher, he told me I had to stop buying filet mignon. He said—"

"I'm coming in on the four-forty-six train at Flatbush Avenue. Are you writing this down?"

"Sure," I lied.

Writing it down where? What did she think I was, a secretary? I was pinned to the furniture. The nearest pad was in the distant past. And a pencil! I hadn't seen a pencil since—

"I want you to meet me at Flatbush Avenue with the financials. Can you do that?"

"I guess."

"But you have to make sure you're not followed."

I burst out laughing.

"It's not funny," she said. "I'm pretty sure he's hired an investigator. He could easily have people watching the house. I would, if I were him."

"Where have you been this whole time?"

"I can't tell you."

"Are you with Ian and Alex?"

"I can't tell you that, either."

She started describing where the files were. I pretended to write things down. I even said, "Uh-huh," and "Wait a minute," as if I was trying to keep up with her.

"Now tell me where you're going to be," she ordered, a boss, having me read back dictation.

"Flatbush Avenue. A train getting in at three-fifty-four."

"Four-forty-six!"

"Right. That's what I meant. Four-forty-six. But I don't get it. If you're coming home, why can't you get these things yourself?"

"I'm not coming home," she snorted. "I can't ever go home again. That's the point. I'm coming in to get the papers, and then I'm leaving again. This is just a handoff."

For the first time, it occurred to me that maybe she wasn't kidding. She hadn't made a single joke since I'd picked up the phone. All our conversations in the past had been jokes, basically, from beginning to end. It was our way of dealing with things. So even though she was acting serious this time, I found it hard to change gears.

"I have to go. Now do you know what to do?"

"Sure." I looked at the imaginary pad, with its already forgotten information fading into invisible pages. "Wait, where exactly do I find the—?"

"See you," she said.

• • •

The apartment was waiting for me. Plants, made dry by steam heat, gratefully soaked up the water I gave them with a loud quenching sound. The refrigerator sprang to life as I came into the kitchen. I ran my finger along a sill. I should have dusted. With a place like mine, so fundamentally dirty, so deep-down chaotic, it didn't matter if you dusted or not. It only made things worse. One patch of clean showed up the filthiness of the rest. But at Marjorie's, even after two months, the dust had formed evenly, different from what it lay on, waiting to be peeled back. You got the sense you could lift it off in one piece.

"Files," I reminded myself.

I let Ann crawl. She'd been getting good at it, lately. She discovered whole new areas, a cluttered forest under the table and among the chairs, a secret corridor behind the toilet and before the wall. She introduced me to strange directions, brutal straight lines that ran right through supposedly fixed objects.

The desk was in the bedroom. I took tax forms, bank statements, stock market stuff. It was all perfectly organized and labeled. Marjorie would need the cat, too, if she was leaving for good. I had seen a traveling case, one of those cages with a handle, in the closet. I got it and sat on the bed.

"Fauntleroy."

He'd only come out that once, but the bowl was always empty. I got up again, filled it, and set it down just beyond the bed. He must be starving. Sometimes, after leaving, I would stand outside the door and listen to his footsteps pitter-patter down the hall, hear the metal shove of his little cat snout driving itself deeper into the stainless-steel dish, pushing it along the floor, his tongue frantically lapping up clean water.

I missed having the dress to work on. Even though it had only taken a week, I felt a deep connection to it. What would I do now, make another? I shook my head. Something fell away and I saw I wasn't a "designer" and never would be. I didn't have it in me. That's what I'd been proving to myself all along. What I *couldn't* do. Beginnings, what felt like beginnings, were really endings. The real beginnings you didn't even notice.

"Fauntleroy," I asked, "where are you?"

I got down and lifted the ruffle that ran around the box spring. Even here, Marjorie had storage containers, wide and flat, with big lids that snapped and sealed shut. Summer sheets. Pillowcases. Something shifted, two eyes, glowing warily, trying to get farther away from me, crouched low.

"Fauntleroy?"

I held out the food dish and rattled it like a beggar.

I was in Ann's world, the underside of objects hitting my head, labels hanging down, surrounded by struts and casters and rug pads.

"Fauntleroy, come out. Here, kitty."

When I looked back, which I was being forced more and more to do, it all seemed inevitable, everything that had happened to me, not like I had any choice at all. And so would this, in twenty years. I'd wonder why I spent all my time being anxious when whatever I was destined to become was just that: destiny. My fate.

"Come here, cat," I said sweetly, and got even lower, on my back, so I could extend my arm as far as it would go. But that wasn't far enough. The bed was huge and I was a small person, stretching my fingertips, realizing there was still an enormous distance left, to where a ball of terrified gray fur plastered itself even tighter against the wall.

It was four o'clock. I brushed myself off and sat again. I had to go. I had to meet the train. I looked down and decided, Starve, you dumb creature.

Just then, I saw his tail. He had come to the edge, drawn by food, and stopped, afraid, thinking he was still safe. But his tail was sticking out, a gray rope. I reached down and grabbed. Instantly, his claws tried to anchor themselves. I hauled him out, hand over fist. He made horrible little meows and hissed at me, but I just shoved him in the box and closed the gate. Then I peered in, trying to for the first time really look at him. But he had made himself invisible, shrinking as far back as he could into the corner.

There was a crash.

I hurried out of the bedroom, lugging the case. Ann had knocked over a box. She was crying, scared by the noise. I picked her up in my other arm and nuzzled her.

"It's all right, it's all right," I murmured.

It hadn't fallen on top of her. She wasn't hurt, just scared. I poked the cardboard with my toe and heard the sickening sound of broken crockery. Marjorie's china.

"It's not your fault. You didn't do anything wrong." I twisted to look at a clock. "But now we have to go."

•   •   •

The elevator was out of service. I held the carrying case away from my body to balance myself while working the stroller down the stairs one step at a time. Fauntleroy kept changing which side of the box he was crouched in, making the three of us sway and tip.

"Isn't this fun?" I said to Ann. "We're at the train station."

I had never been to one with her before. The subway didn't count. Even though it was just a commuter line, there was something about the lit-up board, with its changing destinations, the lines branching out, and all those precise times, that made it special. I loved the announcements, the Arrivals and Departures, the way the places were intoned by an unseen voice.

"Train leaving for Babylon on Track Four, making stops at . . ."

"Babylon," I told Ann.

People flew by. A train pulled in and stopped, completely stopped, blasting air out its brakes. It would never move again. All the doors opened at once. An empty platform was full. We were part of a protected, enclosed, underground world.

"It's OK," I assured both cat and child.

It was one of those rare moments of being very in control and earth-mothery. I had made it to where I was supposed to be, on time, and now all I had to do was wait.

"Well, don't act too excited to see me."

A woman was standing in front of us with dark glasses. She had a scarf on. It covered her hair and knotted under her chin like she had gone out with curlers.

"Hi, Annie."

She knelt down. I wanted to say something, but I was too shaken by her appearance. She had aged, all at once. At first I thought maybe it was her mother, whom I'd never met, a frosted version of Marjorie, with graying hair and powder packing the lines of her face. Even her expressions, what I could make out past the dark glasses and paisley scarf, were an old lady's. The way her mouth cracked open, how her nose seemed pasted on.

"Where are the boys?"

"They're safe. You got your hair cut."

"Is there anyplace we can go? I mean, do you have time, or do you have to . . . ?"

She was staring past me. I turned and looked with her. There was the ticket booth and then a newsstand. A man in a turban stood inside. All the magazines clipped over his head had women in bathing suits.

"Nobody followed me, I don't think." Of course I hadn't been checking. "I mean, you'd have to be an idiot to follow me. Even I wouldn't follow me if I didn't have to. And I'm me! Know what I mean?"

"I'm sorry to freak you out like that," she said. "I know I've been a little crazy."

"A little?"

I was so relieved I wanted to drop everything and give her a hug. She was back, the old Marjorie, my friend. Except it was just a flicker, a reminder of how she used to be.

"Did you get everything?"

"I think so."

She flipped through the files, totally absorbed. We were still standing in the middle of the station. People parted on either side of us. I watched her face. I'd never seen Marjorie look so intently at anything. Her lips were moving. She ran her finger along a line and found something she liked.

"Joint returns," she explained. "A lot of good stuff here."

"Great."

"He doesn't know I made copies."

"So you didn't think you were leaving, the first time. Or you would have taken all this stuff with you, right?"

"The less you know, the better. You may be asked about it someday and I don't want you having to lie."

"I like lying."

"Not under oath, you wouldn't. I can't stay too long."

"What's going *on,* Marjorie? You seem so different."

"I'm not." She was stuffing the files into a soft briefcase I'd never seen before. It wasn't new, though. It was battered and broken in, with a wide flap and little straps that fit into buckles. It looked like it could expand indefinitely. "I'm actually the same. That's what I've discovered. The same as I was before I had kids. I'm back to being me."

"I never knew you then."

"I was a real ball-cutter. That's what Sherman used to call me. We worked at the same firm. Of course he made partner and I didn't. This I don't need."

She handed one file back to me. It was recipes. Typed out. Never used. I must have taken them because they looked the same as the others, all numbers and code. 2 tsp. 4 T. 1½ C.

"Well, I don't want it."

There was a litter basket next to us. She threw it in.

"So what have you been up to?"

Losing it, I wanted to answer. A million different news items presented themselves.

"First of all—"

"I can't let them find me," she went on. "It's crucial, as long as I'm fighting this action in court. It turns out there's a whole network of women who help abused wives."

"Were you abused?"

"Of course I was abused."

It made sense. The sunglasses. The makeup, even. And her fear of being spotted, of my being followed. Although wouldn't her bruises have healed by now?

But she was so much quicker. She saw what I was thinking before I could even put it into words.

"He didn't hit me, Eve. I was emotionally abused."

Coming from her mouth, it was so ugly-sounding. I still pictured her at ease, lounging on a playground bench, eating teething biscuits, unflappable.

"What's that?" She nodded down at the cage. "Are you coming from the vet?"

"No. He's yours." I had forgotten all about Fauntleroy. Now I held him up, so they were at eye level. "Don't you remember? Look."

"You brought the cat?"

"I couldn't leave him there."

"I can't bring a cat. Not where I'm going."

"You mean they don't allow pets?"

She gave the same long sigh the train had made, as if she would never take another step. That's what I was hoping for. I didn't want her to leave. I wanted us to pick up where we left off. Her features, which had been so hard and masklike, softened. She held up the files.

"You did me a real favor today. Thanks."

"What are you going to do with them?"

"I'm going to draft a motion from Hell. And when Sherman reads it—"

"He's going to die?"

"He's going to love it. He used to lie next to me and read my motions in bed. After a full day's work. And laugh. See, when I stopped working, I think he lost respect for me. I know he did. Because I lost respect for myself."

"So you want him back?"

"I haven't even thought that far ahead," she mused. "It's just something to do, right now. Something she *can't* do. It's my way of communicating with him. He doesn't even come to the phone anymore, he's so angry at me. But I know he'll read my briefs. He has to. They're legal documents."

A train was announced. She paused, listening to the long string of towns. I thought I saw her eyes widen, just for a second, at one, but then she concealed it.

"Is that yours?"

"I really don't want you getting involved. How's Harvey?"

"His mother—"

"You know what you need?"

"What?"

"A kick on the ass." She was checking the straps on her bag, preparing to go, jamming the files down. There were a lot more papers. She must have been reading them on the train. Hundreds of them, it looked like. "You don't know how good you've got it. I mean, basically nothing's wrong with you, right? You've got a kid, a husband, you're young—" She looked me over. "I could never figure out why you were so miserable."

"Excuse me," I said, "but I just lugged your cat about twenty blocks."

"I didn't ask you to bring him. I told you, where I'm going—"

"Where *are* you going, anyway? Why won't you say? You think I'm going to tell?"

Her face was all twisted up. She listened to a train announcement, a final call.

"Marjorie?"

"Listen," she sighed. "This isn't working for me. It never was."

"What wasn't working for you?"

"The whole mother-in-the-park thing. I wish it had, but . . . The point is, it *is* working for you, whether you believe it or not. I don't want you to look at what I'm doing as some kind of option."

"I missed you. That's all."

"Well, don't." Even though the bag was meant to go over her shoulder, she hugged it to her chest. "And stop—"

"Stop what?"

"Stop worrying so much," she said kindly.

"That's it?" I asked. "You're going?"

"Wish me luck."

She got on a train. I watched her find a seat. By the time it pulled out, she was already laying papers all around her. She didn't look up to wave.

. . .

Harvey arrived home a robot. He was distracted. Passive. I tried to act as if everything was normal. By ten, we had run out of things to say. He came to the bedroom and stood there. I was watching TV.

"Do we own a cat?"

"Of course."

I could see him searching his mind, trying to remember when he had agreed to that.

"What's his name?"

"Fauntleroy."

"Fauntleroy? You know what Fauntleroy means, don't you?"

"No."

"*Enfant-le-roi.* Child of the king."

"How do you know all this stuff?"

He was still staring. "Do I get to see it?"

"He's under the bed."

He started to get down on his hands and knees.

"Don't bother. He doesn't come out. Except to eat."

He accepted that too. I could have told him anything.

"You know I'm allergic?"

"Oh, yeah." I did remember, vaguely, now that he brought it up. "But all guys say that, don't they? That they're allergic to cats? It's the same as women saying they like jazz."

"You don't like jazz?"

"It's all right," I shrugged.

He nodded.

He was still in shock. I wanted to say, How do you feel? But something in his manner stopped me. He approached everything with a strange deliberation, learning the simplest tasks over, unpacking a suitcase, kissing his daughter. He didn't even notice what was wrong with me. His concern had evaporated. He was too busy mapping out his own hurt.

"You shouldn't change the litter as long as you're still nursing."

"Really? Why?"

"There's a virus that can be passed along in the milk," he said, back in the hallway now. "I'll do it."

"But I was doing it the whole time at—"

Then I realized I'd never told him about the cat at Marjorie's. It was our little secret, mine and Ann's.

"What?"

"Nothing. I stopped nursing," I lied, deciding, at that very moment, to wean her. I was already giving her a few bottles a day. If not now, when? "While you were gone."

"Oh." I could picture him out there, frowning. "You know once you stop, you can't go back."

"I know."

There was a new distance between us. We had agreed, without saying a word, not to mess with each other. We were being polite.

"My breasts are my own," I announced quietly, still watching.

The weatherman was talking about a snow advisory.

"Are you aware there's a large hunk of meat in the refrigerator?"

"That was going to be dinner, but I didn't have time. It turns out you have to cook it for hours. I didn't realize."

"No problem."

"I'll make it tomorrow."

"I'll be here."

So this was it? After everything that happened while he was away, had I ended up becoming even more of a wife than before? Maybe craziness was just a way of blowing off steam so I could act relaxed and composed when it counted. Past the hysteria and paranoia of the past few months, we had reached a low-level stability. We could go on like this forever, existing side by side. And it wasn't so bad. I could handle it. In a sense, it was what I was made for. I changed the channel. I could do two, three, ten things at once. They were all the same. That's what having a kid had taught me. Everything got done, or didn't, and none of it mattered. Like he said, he'd be here tomorrow. And so would I. We were stuck.

"Stuck," I repeated, testing the acoustics.

A quiet came.

But it was all happening too soon! This was premature middle age. The way some people got Early Onset Alzheimer's at fifty or fifty-five, I was already showing signs of the dreaded Zombie-Lardbutt Syndrome before I even hit thirty.

There was one way out. It was really *out*, though, as in beyond the range of rational human behavior. But I didn't care about losing my mind. Maybe there was something better than my mind, underneath. What scared me more was the possibility of losing my soul, of becoming a glazed reflection in the TV's eye. I remembered the story he had told at the restaurant, about the woman who had been raped. Raped and then hypnotized.

"When," Harvey called, "did my underwear turn pink?"

I reached for the phone. I didn't need to look at the slip of paper in my pocket. I had memorized Mark's number.

Chapter Nine

This doesn't change anything, I practiced. I mean, of course it changes everything, but don't think I'm expecting much. We could just meet from time to time, the three of us. You could even take her on outings, I guess, if you want. And then, every once in a while . . .

No. That was wrong.

Let's go back in time, I tried again. You and me. Let's rewrite history.

The storm was different from what I was used to. In the Midwest, it got cold days in advance. Air swept down from the north, gained strength over Canada. It arrived with a special smell, froze the hairs in your nostrils, made a pain behind your forehead. The snow was almost an afterthought. It was the cold that got you.

Here, the wind was warm and wet.

"What *is* this?" I asked Ann, looking straight up at swirling furry flakes.

They were wormy bugs with a million legs, tumbling out of

the sky, disappearing instantly on the sidewalk, where they became a brown-black sludge.

Of course. The eighth plague. Locusts.

My heart was thumping. I was walking faster and faster, making the biggest mistake of my life so far. And yet I was excited. You say something's over. You prove, by making an ass of yourself, that it really is over, then you wake up the next day and it's still there, not over at all.

"I am Dumbo," I realized, finally finding the address.

I remembered our last time in the elevator, on New Year's Eve, how she had been strapped in her stroller. Now, in the Snugli, her little legs kicked to be set free. Soon she would be staggering. I'd seen other kids do it, take their first steps. Soles that barely touched the ground before, never felt the full weight of their body, with its strange shifting center of gravity, take on that life-long balancing act.

"After you walk, you're supposed to fly. You're supposed to flap your wings, which are really your ears, apparently, and become an adult. Don't ask me how. I never saw that movie."

The doors opened. We entered a tropical rain forest. Because it was so messy outside, the contrast was even more striking. The plants had doubled in size. There were buds everywhere. The Gro-Lites beamed their energy right down into the leaves. I unsnapped Ann and got her out of her little cocoon.

Io was wearing the same shoes. I could tell by the banging they made on the floor.

"Here are some towels."

"Thanks."

"It looks terrible out there."

"It's not so bad."

Wooden stakes were driven into each tub at an angle. He did

that right before he harvested. The shock to the root system sent resin rushing up to the leaves. Resin made the buds stronger, more potent. I smiled. The past was coming alive for me, as it had not, for many years.

"I'm making tea."

"That sounds great. Where's—?"

"In back."

She went off in the other direction, to the kitchen.

She wasn't any friendlier than last time, but no worse, I decided. It was just her manner. Anyway, I wasn't here to see Io.

Ann didn't go anywhere at first, just checked out her new surroundings, getting in touch with its invisible forces. I took a deep breath, nervous. Then she began to crawl. She'd picked up his scent.

I rehearsed a third and final speech.

I want you to save my marriage by occasionally reminding me of who I am, or who I used to be. You can shower Ann in your love, and if you just let a little of that love come my way too, that's all I need. That's all I want. From you.

We broke through the last row of plants to the braided rug and lamp where I'd first met Io. But the big chair had been pushed aside and there were people sitting on the floor, women, six or seven of them, all young, without babies.

"Was he actually a shark? Or was she just hallucinating?"

"He was the spirit of a shark. He could turn into a shark at will."

"No, he *was* a shark. He could turn into the surfer dude at will."

"But only for short periods of time. His essential nature was that of a shark, wasn't it?"

Nobody was quite sure.

"But when they were in the water together, it seemed like—"

"That's where I was confused too. Especially when she feels that fin growing out of his back."

"Hi there!"

Because they were all low down, they saw Ann first.

"Hello! Who are you?"

My eyes swept past them—they were so irrelevant—looking for Mark. He must be here somewhere. Ann had paused too, as puzzled as I was, but then saw a plate of cookies in the middle of the rug and starting crawling again, all elbows and knees.

"Isn't she cute?"

"Ann, no!" I said, in my Awful Voice.

Years before, for no reason, I had found a copy of *Dog Training for Dummies,* which I now realized was where most of my parenting ideas came from.

"Oh, can't she have just one?"

They had tippy little teacups, which they didn't know enough to keep their hands on. She had already knocked one over. The whole area was a minefield. I stepped in the middle and scooped her up before she reached the platter. She started to cry.

Io appeared behind us.

"It's herbal. I hope you don't mind."

"That's great," I said, trying to make the grip I had her in look like a warm motherly hug instead of a wrestling hold. I was desperately looking around, seeing if we could somehow get past these strangers, keep moving to that different part of the loft where he was waiting for us.

"Everyone, this is Eve and . . ."

"Ann."

"Of course. Ann. Sit over here. Next to me."

Oh, shit! I almost answered, seeing they all had the same

paperback he had brought that night. It was the book club. When Io had said, "Why don't you come over Saturday morning?" I thought that was because Mark would definitely be here, that he wouldn't be out on some job, not because it was when her stupid I-Have-Time-to-Read discussion group met.

"This is Ginny, Christine, Debby . . ."

The company of women. Which was supposed to be so restorative. I settled on the floor with that uncomfortable feeling of trying to fit in to something you know you can't wear anymore, the persona of a single girl, all these hopes and dreams it was just assumed you shared. It used to terrify me that either they sincerely did, and I was left out, a fraud, faking my way through life, or none of us really believed what we'd been taught, that it was a universally accepted lie, and the main reason we gathered was to reinforce each other's delusions, those myths everything pointed us toward: that we would find that special someone, that we would in some unspecified way succeed, that we would be fulfilled.

"Where do you guys know each other from?" I asked.

They looked around, as if they weren't quite sure.

"School, mostly."

I was far from that now, even in terms of appearance. It wasn't that they were all pretty, but even the least pretty of them was still putting out this aura of availability. Io and I were the only ones not dressed up. And she's married, I remembered. A quick survey of everyone else's fingers told me we were the only two. So I actually had more in common with her.

She sat cross-legged on the floor. Her jeans rode up. She wasn't wearing socks.

"What's that?"

"What's what? Oh, a tattoo."

I looked more closely. It wasn't really a tattoo, not of anything. It was more of a blur, a band of color going around her ankle.

"Did you read the book, Eve?"

"Some of it."

"We were talking about when Kaz turns into a shark."

The heat was making noise, that steady background sound that makes you think for a minute you're tuned to a cosmic frequency, the key the whole universe is vibrating in, but then you realize is just air. Io was in a sleeveless goosedown vest. She was so resolutely unsexy. Except she had on earrings, I noticed. Fancy ones with what looked like real diamonds.

"Where's Mark?"

"Up there."

She nodded to the ceiling. I looked and saw we were under a skylight, and then remembered he wasn't allowed to smoke down here, most of the time.

"On the roof, you mean? Isn't he getting wet?"

Does he know I'm coming? was what I really wanted to ask. Does he know I'm here now? With an offer that will change his life?

"He has an umbrella."

"Oh."

"Well, what could she have done?" someone was arguing. "I mean, he was perfectly fine as long as there was no blood in the water."

Ann was hungry, blindly head-butting my chest. I had a bottle of formula in the bag. It was hot when I made it but had cooled off during the walk down. I shook it and felt Io watching.

"I could get him," she offered. "I have this stick I use, to bang on the glass."

"No. Never mind. Do you want to do this?"

I held out the bottle. She stared at it for a minute.

"OK."

I helped get Ann settled in her lap, then gave her the formula. She was awkward at first, concentrating.

"Just hold it like . . . that's right."

She tilted the bottle too far over. Ann coughed and sputtered. I put my hand on hers and guided it back to the right angle.

"Look. See the bubbles? That's how you know it's working."

I had that sympathetic reaction, a physical twinge, as if I was still nursing. All these invisible ties, I thought. Everyone caught in webs of feeling.

"I've been meaning to tell you something." She talked, not quite in a whisper, but in a very flat, private tone that was meant just for me, not for people even an extra foot away. "It wasn't exactly true. What I told you before, at the party, about how we met."

She stared down at Ann.

"Really?" I asked, just to be polite, and edged closer.

"I took this self-defense class for women." She still wasn't making eye contact, speaking even more quietly, while everyone else talked about the book. "What to do in case, you know."

"Sure."

"And the instructor— I don't know where she knew him from, but Mark was there."

"I don't understand. Mark was taking a class in women's self-defense?"

"He was the example. The attacker. He was the one she demonstrated on."

"Oh. He does like to volunteer."

I remembered him posing for us, that first time. How he came out from behind a screen. The first naked body I had ever seen. In that way. With beauty first and lust coming after. Instead of how it usually was, desire knocking you over and then finding the beauty, frantically looking for it, convincing yourself it existed, as a way of justifying what you were feeling.

"He's very community-oriented," she agreed.

I looked to see if she was joking.

"So what did he do?"

"Well, he would approach, from either in front or behind, and you'd have to kind of fend him off, with all these moves you were supposed to have learned."

The cover of the book was on the floor in front of us. It had a Polynesian-looking guy wearing a tiny bathing suit, seen in profile, holding a surfboard in front of him, with that curving, hooked rudder that sticks out the bottom corresponding to just about where his penis would be, if his penis was eleven inches long and shaped like a triangle.

"Sounds kinky."

"No. He was very professional. He showed me what to do in different situations, if I was grabbed or choked. Whatever was supposed to be happening."

"And that's when you got together."

"Not really." She flipped her hair. It was a gesture that didn't go with anything I'd seen in her before. Haughty and upper-class. Her diamonds glittered. "It was just how we started to talk. When I found out what he did, that he was a contractor, I told him my parents needed work done on their house. And that's where we really got to know each other. But it's not like I met him there. Which is what I said before."

"And why exactly are you telling me this?"

"I don't like having lies between us. Not with people I care about. That's something I've learned from therapy."

"Well . . . thanks," I said uncertainly.

Ann shifted and Io shifted with her, getting more comfortable.

I looked at her ankle again and saw, as the border of the tattoo became more exposed, what it was supposed to be: the fluorescent pink spray paint he marked his tool handles with, so they wouldn't be lost or stolen on a job, so they wouldn't get mixed up with someone else's.

"Kaz Kala-KU-au? Or Kaz Kala-ku-AU?" somebody wondered.

He's hiding from me, I realized. He doesn't want to come down.

I tried to peer up through the skylight, maybe make out a shadow holding an umbrella, a silhouette smoking a joint, staring out over the rooftops, waiting for us to finish. But all I could see was snow.

"I don't want there to be lies with someone I'm *friends* with," she went on, still looking away from me, down at the bottle.

. . .

We left before the others. Ann got restless. Io had put our coats on the radiator, so they were dry.

"Thanks for inviting me. I had fun."

"If you want to go up on the roof, there's another staircase, past the last landing."

"No, that's all right. Tell him I said hello."

Mark wasn't the answer. I didn't know when it had become

clear, but sometime during the afternoon I had made up my mind. I felt more of a bond with Io, linked by our shared feeling. She could deal with Mark, now. Alone. He was her problem.

"There's something we've been meaning to ask you. Both of us."

"What?"

"It's a favor you could do. But if you want to, you can say no. It's OK."

"Anything," I said.

I was feeling generous, hoisting Ann back into the Snugli, resuming my burden. This had been a nice break, this flight of fancy. Now I could handle whatever came my way. She opened the door to the loft—I'd never been on the stairs before, only ridden up in the elevator—and led us out, as if we couldn't discuss whatever it was inside her home.

"He told you, right?"

"Told me what?"

"About kids. How I can't have them?"

"He might have said something," I answered, not sure how much I was supposed to know.

Everything on the landing was creaky and dusty. It was still a factory out here, not renovated yet. The paint on the square banisters, just big sawed-off lengths of wood, was thick and gray. You could sense years of layers underneath. The light was almost black. When you looked up, the walls disappeared in darkness.

"It really sucks."

"I'm sorry. Have you tried—?"

"There are these women you can hire. But the contracts aren't legally binding. So half the time they just disappear. Or else they hold you up for more money. Plus, you never know if they're really taking care of themselves, the whole time. They could be doing drugs. They *all* smoke, all of them. And you know they're not going to quit. In general, they're poor and unreliable."

"Wait a minute."

"So they say you should use a sister. Or a cousin. But I don't have any of those. I come from a small family. And none of Mark's sisters are interested."

"I don't really get what you're talking about, Io."

"We want you to be our birth mother."

"You want me to be what?"

"We want you to carry our baby."

"I already have a baby." Whom I'm already carrying, in case you hadn't noticed, I wanted to add.

I still didn't really understand what she was saying. I mean, the conscious answering part of my brain did, but not the place inside where things connect with each other and supposedly make sense.

"Well, that's the point. The odds are less that you'd have any sort of complication. And of course it's much easier the second time."

"What is?"

"Delivery."

"Oh."

"We'd pay for everything. My parents would. It wouldn't even be in a hospital. There's a clinic on Park Avenue."

"You know," I said, "I lied too. Before."

She actually had a brochure. She was taking it out of her back pocket. So this was all a trap. A setup.

"About the charcoal sketch, I mean. The one I made of Mark, that first time."

"It has these birthing suites where there's a pool of warm

water and special lighting and even your choice of music. You can bring your own, or they have a selection. There's rock, folk, light classical—"

"I didn't draw his penis. I traced it."

She looked up, puzzled.

"With my tongue."

"I really don't want to know this, Eve."

"But there shouldn't be any lies between us, right? Otherwise it's not"—I reached back and, for once, found the perfect word—"therapeutic."

"Will you at least look at the brochure?"

"No, I will not look at the brochure."

"We'd pay you a fee, of course. Or get you something. A car. Or a bigger apartment. My father owns a few buildings in—"

"Go fuck yourself!"

*   *   *

The wind had changed direction. It was snowing *up,* hitting me under the chin. I couldn't figure out which way to go. I wasn't familiar with the neighborhood. Clumps of sleet were pelting me from different sides. I got confused and headed downhill because it was easier, because that's where my momentum took me, but also to shield Ann, who was trying to burrow deeper into my coat.

"When the snow did come, it stayed," I resumed, telling her my memories of Iowa winter. "Flakes multiplied on the ground. A few inches became a foot. And then more. One foot became three, instantly. It was never less than knee-high. And when the sun finally reappeared, it was weak and distant, melting the tops of the drifts so they would harden again in thin layers that supported you for maybe a few magical seconds, if you were light enough, if you were young enough—"

I remembered a glimpse of soft, untouched, rolling glitter.

"—before breaking under your feet and trapping each leg. Getting anywhere was impossible. Grown-ups complained, but not me. You could eat it. You could scoop your hand deep down and pull out a lump of white that tasted like nothing else. It was so pure."

My foot got soaked in a freezing puddle.

"Not like here," I muttered.

I had this recalculating to do, re-seeing all our encounters since we had met each other that day in the playground. I was aware of how my body had played a trick on me, put itself in a mode it had no business being in, how it had convinced me there was all this evidence he was interested in me again when really, when really—

"When really he's a jerk," I pointed out. "A jerk, a weakling, and a coward."

So that's why Io had wanted him to get close to me again. They had talked. They had used me. And he hadn't come down from the roof today because he knew what she was going to ask and didn't want to be around for it. He let her do his dirty work.

We stayed close to old warehouses being transformed into stores, to posters and plywood in front of suddenly gaping lots where new condos would go up. Ann was dragging me down. She was too big to be carried, but the stroller was impossible in this weather. Besides, it felt right to suffer, not to let go. After all these months of wondering what I could do, the answer had finally been presented to me. I had found my calling at last, the only thing I was qualified for.

Baby maker.

The street ended in a wide pier that looked up to Lower Manhattan. Definitely the wrong direction, I registered mechanically. Snow was accumulating on my eyelashes and shoulders. I pictured myself white and stooped over. I hadn't pulled that aging trick on myself yet, but now I felt it coming, all at once, a wrecking ball swinging through my stomach. Skyscrapers stuck up, spearing the slop as it fell. I waited to cross the last road. A few cars hurried past with sooty carbon-monoxide-soaked chunks of ice hanging down behind their wheels.

"We should go home," I whispered.

At the edge of the pier, I watched the flakes dissolve in water. They weren't falling, they were returning. It could snow as much as it wanted into the harbor and the level wouldn't rise one inch. The steady breathing of the swells would take it in, restore it to some pristine natural state.

You'd think the railing would be taller, part of me went on, trying to fill in the silence that reigned in my soul. To prevent people from jumping. Like on top of the Empire State Building.

Instead, it was absurdly small, the way all barriers are when you're already past them, in your mind.

The wind swung around. I slipped and righted myself. Everything was icing over. The storms here came from the south, dumped their moisture, then arctic air froze it in place and immortalized the mess.

Even though the railing was low, I had a hard time getting over. Like climbing *out* of something, a bathtub or a pit. But I did it—and in that one little step saw more: what was hidden if you stayed safely on the other side. There were rocks, huge boulders shoring up the foundation. Water lapped at the spaces in between, filled and emptied all the gaps so unthinkingly, so invitingly.

I stood there, entranced. What was this? The ocean, of course. I'd never been this close. The ocean that surrounded the frail outcropping of sanity we all clung to. I took another step. It was such a relief to leave flat surfaces, the boring predictable geography we paved over our dreams with. Here, everything was drastically altered. You really felt gravity pulling at you, and what you heard was the munch of waves, an unseen digestion eating away at the certainty of everyday life. I kicked a pebble loose and watched it bounce once, twice, then fly high off the final part of the jetty, disappear noiselessly out of time and space forever. Not even a *plop*. If only I could slip out of the world the same way, without making a tear in the fabric of things, find a secret opening in the surface that would close seamlessly behind, as if I had never been. I took another step.

Something hit me. The force pushed us forward. My boots slid on the icy rocks. I reached back and found a hand to hold on to, but it gave and came with me. We both fell together, our combined weight sliding down onto the sharp rocks, each kicking, trying to dig in our heels, until we stopped, inches before the steep drop-off.

"What are you doing?" I screamed.

I had one arm around Ann, who was half out of her Snugli, and one on what turned out to be the sleeve of Harvey's jacket.

"Me?" he asked. "What am *I* doing?"

"You pushed me."

"I was trying to grab you."

"Why would you do that?"

"I thought—"

"You could have gotten us killed!"

We couldn't move. We were close to the edge but tangled up so much that, even now, it was impossible to get free.

"Is she all right?"

I looked down my chest.

"I think so."

"Good."

We lay there a minute, catching our breaths, trying to figure out what had happened. The city, that ever-present sense you had of it grinding you down, was gone. Urban life was behind us. I stuck out my tongue and let some snow melt on it, tasting the same taste I had just been remembering from before, almost metallic, more of an awareness. Harvey's leg lay across me. His hand was still gripping my forearm, which ached. I could tell I was going to be bruised all over.

"Shhh," I told Ann.

"I thought you were going to—"

"I was just looking at the water. You almost knocked me in. What are you doing here, anyway?"

"Following you."

"Oh, great." I thought back to all the time I'd been in the loft. "You mean for the last hour and a half you've been shivering in a doorway?"

I tried to look over and see if he was all right, but even that made us slide a little farther down.

"Stay still!"

"All right, all right! You don't have to yell."

For the first time it occurred to me that we might actually be in trouble. It had all seemed so benign, the edge, even a foot away. But in our heavy wet clothes, and me with Ann, it would be hard to climb back out. And there was absolutely no one here.

"Don't be afraid, Eve."

"I'm not afraid. I'm pissed off."

He gave a little laugh.

"Didn't you trust me? It was a book club group, for crying out loud. I wasn't cheating on you. And even if I was, I certainly wouldn't take Ann with me. What kind of a sick twisted creature do you think I am?"

"You thought I'd taken her with me," he pointed out, "when you saw us together with Mindy, remember? I figured maybe you were doing the same exact thing. Just like you did before, that time you went to Coney Island."

He was right. Was that what we'd been doing? Testing each other? Punishing each other for imagined wrongs?

"Can I take my arm away?" he asked.

"You can try. But keep your leg there."

Slowly, he detached himself, just enough to turn so he could face me.

"I thought you were going to fall."

"I told you, I was just looking."

"That's all it takes. You look too long, you fall in."

I tore my eyes away from the water. Yes, it was mesmerizing but not, ultimately, where I wanted to be. Some of the buildings were beginning to turn on their signal lights, the ones to warn off airplanes, even though it was early afternoon. The storm made it look later in the day. Harvey's cheeks were red.

"You've been outside a long time."

"It wasn't so bad."

"You shouldn't be jealous. You've got nothing to be jealous about."

"I wasn't jealous. I was worried."

I wanted to reach out and touch him, touch his frozen face, but for that I'd need the third hand I kept imagining I'd grown. The other two were busy holding my daughter and myself.

"Worried *and* jealous," he admitted. "And everything else."

"Really? Because you always act like nothing's wrong."

"Of course things are wrong. I'm falling apart."

"You are?"

"But when you're not around, I can't show it. I can't show any-thing."

"I've been around."

"No, you haven't. I would know, if you were. You're the path-way all my feelings come through."

"If I'm so important to you, then how come we never make love anymore?"

He looked puzzled, as if he'd never connected the two, which I must admit I never had either, but as soon as I said it, it made sense. It was like he said: Sex was a ritual, an enactment of who we were, what we meant to each other. And for so long it hadn't been happening. I leaned forward, clutched Ann to my chest, and craned my head around her body to kiss him on the lips. I found that extra limb, which was just love, plain old boring love, and suddenly felt more secure, more stable.

"I don't know why." He was fumbling for an explanation, even though, to me, just asking the question had solved the problem. "At first, it was that you hurt, that you were so physi-cally beat up from having her. And then you were so unhappy. I felt responsible, that I had gotten you into something you didn't want. I thought I had trapped or tricked you into becom-ing a—"

"Oh, please," I interrupted. "Into becoming a mother? You make it sound like it was all your idea. You didn't trap or trick me into anything. I knew exactly what I was doing."

"No, you didn't. It was an accident."

I shook my head. "That's what I've had such trouble accept-ing, these last few months. I *wanted* this."

"You did?"

I could feel tears melting channels in the ice of my face. I started telling him everything that had happened, everything I had done wrong or imagined I had done wrong, although when I said it out loud it didn't really amount to much. It was mostly in my head. What else is there left to confess to? I wondered, as the anxiety poured out of me. I described breaking up with Mark that last time and going right to the clinic—so much for trapping or tricking me into becoming a mother—through going to the Gramercy Park Hotel and practically throwing myself at Martin Cooper, to what had happened just now, at the loft. I didn't want to stop because he had gotten so quiet and still. He was listening hard and frowning.

"I didn't even get you a present," I sobbed, sprinkling over the mass apology with a few last petty regrets.

"Eve—"

"For our anniversary, I mean. I was going to, that day, but then instead I stole that piece of—"

"Eve," he said impatiently, "will you just stop talking?"

He looked not old, not young, but his own age, precisely. And I probably did too.

"What did you tell her?" he asked.

"Tell who?"

"Io. About having their baby."

"Oh. I told her . . . thanks but no thanks."

He looked at me.

"Well, maybe I got a little angry. But that's all right. There's plenty of cursing in the Bible. You just have to imagine how things sounded back then. 'A generation of vipers.' 'Godless heathen.' Even 'O ye of little faith,' if you update it, is probably more like, You pathetic little excuse for a—"

"I like it when you stand up for yourself," he said.

"You do?"

"It makes me proud."

I thought about that for a minute. Or did the opposite of thinking. I let thought stop, for one blessed mini-eternity, and emerged refreshed. There was a blissful relief. An unknotting.

"What I don't understand, though, is why you've been so miserable. If you say you wanted this all along."

"I did, but . . . the problem is, I don't know if I want the right things."

"Of course you do. You wanted me." He said it like it was an accepted fact. "And I'm the right thing for you."

"And you wanted me," I said slowly.

He nodded.

I moved her between us. The signals on the tops of buildings blinked on and off, their colors smearing in the snow. We held each other. A wave of exhaustion came over me.

"I've been depressed."

"No shit."

"But I think I'm better."

He looked around, as if to indicate our surroundings didn't exactly support my claim.

"Well, I'm definitely not going to get any worse."

"Prove it."

I brushed the snow from his thick eyebrows. Something stirred inside me.

"Can we go home now?"

• • •

But we didn't do it right away. The cold and wet left us both sick for about ten days. We spent a strange, dreamy time, half awake, half dressed, taking care of each other and of her, locking the door, closing the bedroom curtains, shutting out the world completely. We shivered and coughed and starved. We were very careful and attentive. It was like after a forest fire, when the green begins to creep back.

One day, I felt well enough to go to the corner store. Tottering up and down the aisles, my body instructed me what to buy. A vitamin deficiency guided my eyes, made me salivate uncontrollably at things I wouldn't ordinarily consider. I came home with a bag of oranges, two bowling-ball-sized grapefruits, and a pineapple.

"Is this some kind of diet?" Harvey asked.

"I think we're already on one, just from not eating."

"Fasting and prayer?" he smiled.

We peeled oranges and watched the citrus oil from the skins burst into the air. They smelled so good. Ann was asleep. After we ate, we went into the bedroom.

"I forgot to tell you. While you were away, I finally saw the cat."

"Fauntleroy? He came out?"

"Just for a few minutes."

"Does that mean winter's almost over?"

"He's a cat, Eve. Not a groundhog."

I noticed he was staring at me.

"What?" I asked. "Is something wrong?"

"Did you get a haircut?"

"You finally noticed. Yes. About three weeks ago."

He took my hands and lazily pinned them to the bed. I had forgotten how strong he was. His full weight, his soft brown eyes, poised over me.

"It looks good," he murmured.

I struggled, hard, just to luxuriate in how firmly I was caught.

•   •   •

Mindy's waiting room was worse than usual. There were children with fevers, runny noses, hacking juicy coughs. One horribly deformed boy had an earlobe blown up to the size of a small balloon.

"Eve."

She cut through it all, in her white lab coat. No baby's going to throw up on *me,* her manner seemed to say.

"We're running a little late. I had them give you the last appointment of the day, so we can talk, after."

"Why? Is everything—?"

"Everything's fine. I just wanted you to know it's going to be a little bit of a wait. Is that all right?"

"Sure."

Even a month ago, I would have been filled with dread at the prospect of having to entertain Ann for so long, but lately either she had gotten easier or I had gotten better at dealing with her.

"How old is your daughter?"

It was the mother of the boy with the ear. I tried not to stare, but could see another place now, on his cheekbone, that had the same gross puffy area, a bubble of flesh so stretched out it sagged and jiggled, then a third, farther down, on his chin.

"Nine months. What about him?"

"A year and a half."

She touched his head, proud. He would take a few steps and fall after every third one, then pop up again. So it wasn't just on the surface, whatever had happened. It was deep down and unfixable.

"Alan," she said, "see the little girl?"

I tried not to clutch Ann, although that was my shameful instinct, to protect her from whatever he had.

"You're waiting to see Dr. Cole?"

I nodded.

"She's wonderful, isn't she?"

"Oh, yes."

"We moved out of the city but we still come in to see her, because Alan likes her the best of all the doctors, doesn't he?"

The boy's expression was a cruel parody of thought, a deep puzzlement that never went away.

"She's so giving. Don't you think?"

"Right," I said.

We talked a bit more, the usual empty politeness, which was even more obscene since it was really about ignoring the heartbreaking tragedy right in front of us. They got called in last. She let him walk down the hall by himself. He hit the floor as if it was part of his natural motion, popping back up again each time, a rubber ball. It took too long, though. Halfway there, I caught just a hint of exasperation, what her life was really like, as she whisked him off his feet and carried him the rest of the way.

* * *

"Any problems?" Mindy asked.

"I don't know." I was determined to sound more responsible than last time. "She seems a little low energy."

"Lethargic?"

"I guess."

She shone a flashlight in Ann's eyes, then each ear.

"How about you?"

"Me? I'm fine."

"Hold her." She placed Ann in my lap, then started listening to her heart, pressing different parts of her body.

"I mean, I guess I'm doing fine. As far as I can tell. What about Harvey? How do you think he's doing?"

I tried to make it sound like a casual question, filling up the small space of the room with talk while she did her exam.

"Harvey?"

"You guys still run into each other, don't you?"

"Not lately." She took off her stethoscope. "I owe you an apology."

"No, you don't."

"I'm sorry about that whole . . . misunderstanding, before. I thought I was acting in your best interests, but clearly I wasn't. I should have told you right away what was going on."

"Maybe not. I was pretty screwed up."

"Not as screwed up as me."

She unclipped her hair, let it fall around her shoulders, then gathered it up again and pulled it back tight.

"You? Mindy, you're the least screwed-up person I know."

"I was really crazy about him. All through school."

"Harvey? You were?"

She nodded.

"I'm sorry."

"Don't be."

She went back to looking at Ann. There was an awkward silence.

"What about her?" I tried ignoring what I'd just heard, even though I knew I'd treasure it, later, as proof that I had not been totally insane, that there was a germ of truth in even the most paranoid suspicions. "Is there anything wrong?"

"Not that I can see. It's possible her 'low energy' is just you coming to accept the fact that it's finally stopped."

"What's finally stopped?"

"The colic. That often happens around now. They quiet down."

"Wait a minute. You mean you don't even know what it was in the first place, and now you're saying it's gone away? For no reason?"

"Children are mysterious creatures."

She smiled and ran a finger down the middle of Ann's chest. I'd never seen her show affection toward a baby before. Usually she just had a sort of clinical interest.

"I got to get me one of these," she said.

It was dark in the hallway. The receptionist must have forgotten about us. We were beyond the last patient, in a post-medical world. The empty office was spooky. No more screaming. No more cures, either. Mindy walked ahead to turn on a light.

"That boy who went in before us. With the ear? Is he going to be all right?"

She didn't answer for a moment.

"It depends on what you mean by 'all right.' But the simple answer is no. That's a very serious condition."

"How could you live with something like that?"

"The mother, you mean? You'd be amazed."

"At what?"

"Oh . . . love. Where people find it. What incredible reserves of strength it gives them. It's one of the neat things about this job. Seeing that."

We left her on the street in front of the building. I didn't know if I should wait for a bus or take the subway. Finally, I decided to walk. I wrapped my arms around Ann as we passed through all the neighborhoods. Cobble Hill. Boerum Hill. Gowanus. And then our own, Park Slope. Real places. With real people. I had never felt a part of them, until now. I was hugging her fiercely.

"You'd better be worth it," I whispered.

. . .

The next day, Ann and I checked out the playground. It was surprisingly warm in the sun. I settled down on the other side, where the older mothers sat. About a half hour later, Alison showed up. She parked next to us.

"I saw you here and just had to come over. God, Dominic woke me up before he left and I am just *dripping* with him."

"Which Dominic?"

"Very funny."

She was—I couldn't say back to normal, I didn't know what normal was for Alison—but less high-strung than that last time in front of the hardware store. She acted like nothing had happened. Both our kids crawled up to a patch of icy snow. The sun was strong. Without any leaves on the trees, everything was revealed, caught in a flash of lightning that wouldn't go away.

"So what are you doing today?"

"We can only stay for a minute. We're on our way to Movement Class."

"What's that?"

"It's this indoor thing. Dominic crawls through all these tunnels and then he does tumbling to music."

"Sounds like a nightmare."

"Not really. You have to follow them around the course, so it's exercise for you too."

I looked at her, trying not to laugh.

"I know, it's a little ridiculous. I signed up for it when I was on these pills. He likes it, though."

"What pills?"

"Oh, they make you happy. But I stopped taking them after a while. I decided happiness wasn't all it's cracked up to be. They did lift me out of this rut I was in. But they also killed my sex drive, which was a problem. And I found myself collecting all these gardening implements, for some reason." She yawned. "Sorry I'm talking so much. I quit smoking."

"Again?"

"Still! It's been a year."

"Wow."

"Anyway, I'm here," she finished, as if this was this logical endpoint she'd been driving at, careening toward, the whole time.

We sat and watched. Ann and Dominic were cautiously touching the ice. Their knees and palms were black from the rubber play surface.

"What about you?"

"I'm well," I pronounced carefully.

"You look like you've lost weight."

"I was sick."

She nodded.

Other mothers came. There was this general thaw. As soon as you moved into the shade it was still freezing, though. I smiled and closed my eyes. A breeze rushed past my ears.

"Dominic!"

"What?" I asked, jerked awake.

She was gathering her things.

"Time to go!"

I squinted down at the ground.

"Look at your fingers, Eve. Don't you have gloves?"

"I had . . . some mittens. Ages ago. But I lost them, I don't remember where."

She took off her pair, which were really furry, put her hands on mine, and squeezed to warm them up. She was wearing that Tibetan hat again. Its woolen balls tickled my face.

"A year without smoking." I swallowed. Was it possible she was wearing perfume? The memory of the kiss came back. "That's a long time. Congratulations."

"Still don't know what to do with my *mouth*," she said, and shot me a look.

* * *

"Now that woman is trouble," I told Ann. We watched them leave. Alison wasn't dressed like she was on her way to a charity fund-raiser anymore. Instead, she was wearing incredibly tight jeans. "But she could be a friend, I guess."

A cloud passed in front of the sun. I shivered and rubbed my hands together, trying to keep some of her warmth.

"You make do with what's available. It's like you're tossed on a beach and have to build a whole new life out of what you've been shipwrecked with."

Ann looked up.

I saw, or imagined I saw, an actual expression, although I couldn't say an expression of what. More a contortion of the face. Except it reminded me of someone. It reminded me of *her*. Was that possible, that she was beginning to be a person?

"I guess it's just you and me now."

I waited for her to answer and, when she didn't, went on.

"There are things I have to tell you. But you can't understand yet. And even after you can understand, you won't really get what I'm saying until you run into the same situation in your own life. And by then I won't be around. Or I'll be this stick figure you can't share your troubles with. This person you're in flight from. That's what makes the whole idea of talk so meaningless."

To prove my point, she had crawled away in the middle of what I was saying.

"Still, I guess it's what I'll be doing, for the next fifty years or so. There has to be *more*, though. Doesn't there? A way to leave you a message."

"This isn't Kyle, is it?"

"It sure is."

"He's gotten so big! Look at you, Kyle!"

"Hello, Allegra. I just love your scarf."

I reached down into the bag, groping for something to do. Maybe I felt more comfortable here, but I wasn't ready to have one of those playground conversations.

"Did your shoe come off? Are you walking around without a shoe? Poor little thing!"

My fingers closed around a solid edge at the very bottom and fished it out. The journal. I'd been lugging it around this whole time. There was still a pencil stuck between its pages. I flipped back over what little I'd done so far, the letter starting off to no one, the clumsy dress designs, and then, on the very first page, the scratches of a creature who hadn't even been able to form a simple sentence.

"Adrian! Oh, honey, that's not safe. Come back here, please."

In the sandbox, Ann was exploring.

"Adrian, come down here this instant!"

An airplane was passing overhead. Martin Cooper, I imagined, flying south to Morocco. The sun blinded me, and when I looked back down again everything was different. I was starry-eyed. There was a yellow fuzz on the bushes beyond the fence.

Words appeared.

Not the words I had once waited for on the pregnancy test stick, but words on a page, one after the other. My daughter was pushing sand together, piling it high.

"Pot roast for dinner tonight," I reminded myself, picking up the pencil.

And got to work.

Parallel Play

Thomas Rayfiel

A Reader's Guide

An Interview with Thomas Rayfiel

Question: As a male writer burrowing into a young mother's head, what kind of research did you undertake? Was the advice of female friends and family members a crucial factor in conceiving the book?

Thomas Rayfiel: My research consisted of caring for two screaming babies (now delightful children). In certain purely technical matters, my wife and other women have corrected me, but I'm a firm believer that we spend too much time focusing on how different men and women are. There are so many "male" and "female" qualities in each of us. To wall them off or suppress them is to deny who we are.

Q: Eve often seems to loathe motherhood and to lack a loving bond with her baby daughter. Is the downside of motherhood a taboo you were keen to address? Are there more resentful, bewildered mothers out there than we'd like to think?

TR: Eve doesn't loathe motherhood or lack a loving bond with Ann. She loathes being expected to feel all these things she isn't ready to admit exist in her, yet. When she finally does, I would argue her love is deep and true and real. It is earned. I do think parents (women, in particular) are given this impossible standard to live up to and that it can cause feelings of inadequacy and craziness when their feelings don't match the saccharine cliché that society holds up as being "normal."

Q: Who are your inspirations? Do you read a lot while you are writing? Do you have any anxieties of influence?

TR: My main inspiration when I sit down to work is the last sentence I wrote the day before, to figure out where it came from and so to see where the next one is going. Of course, getting that very first sentence, the one containing the DNA for all that follows, is the tough part.

Reading is a great part of my life, and yes, I read books while I write. There's probably some dynamic between what I'm reading and what I'm writing, but it's not a conscious one. I don't "bone up" on a subject. As for "anxieties of influence," do you mean am I afraid of sounding like someone else? No. For better or worse, I'm me.

Q: Beyond wanting to continue Eve's story from the previous two novels (*Colony Girl, Eve in the City*), was there a particular spark that got this novel going—a specific theme or scene?

TR: Yes, the dawning realization that women have been sold a bill of goods about motherhood, assured they will instantly fall in love with their newborn child and their newfound lot. I noted it not to be so and, speaking to mothers, saw the feeling was widespread: the sharp and funny minds of former lawyers, editors, and artists pretending they were just as content earnestly debating the pros and cons of various brands of disposable diapers or mushed-up carrots. That suggested comic possibilities, the alternative being to blow one's brains out.

Q: Did you set out to investigate the possibilities and illusions of free will with this book? Do you think that parenthood changes one's perceptions of free will?

TR: I do think parenthood makes you realize that many of the so-called choices offered to you are not really choices at all. You can choose, but the "you" doing the choosing is subject to all sorts of social and biological imperatives. Every move you make is either conforming or reacting to some external or internal expectation. As Eve says, at one of her bleakest moments, "It made me feel I was on a sled, going downhill. Sure, I could lean a little from side to side and maybe influence where I went, to the right a few feet or to the left, give it my own personal style, but basically my future was already decided." The key, as she discovers, is to choose something that isn't offered, to create her own path with her own feet, as she begins to do by the end.

Q: The fact that Eve is known by a single, scripturally resonant name could signal her as an elemental or archetypal woman. Did you intend Eve to be a symbol as well as a fully rounded character?

TR: Honestly? I just liked the name. I also liked the associations of her always being "on the eve" of something, teetering on some brink.

Q: Eve can be selfish and insensitive. Is there a thrill for you in dancing on the thin line between humanizing a deeply flawed character and creating an unlikable heroine?

TR: I don't see Eve as any more selfish or insensitive than other people. What she is, because of her outsider upbringing, is more coldly honest and critical about her own shortcomings. (She's also open to all sorts of mystical currents our mainstream upbringing has numbed us to.) I think we all tend to gloss over certain unpleasant truths about ourselves because, well, otherwise it's tough to get through the day. But Eve is like one of those kids they find in the forest who's been raised by wolves. Her take on things is bracingly honest and, I hope, funny.

Q: *Parallel Play* is written in a confessional first-person voice and set in a domestic milieu, and thus on a superficial level, it bears comparison to certain "chick-lit" novels and popular memoirs of motherhood, almost all of them written by women. Which of these books, if any, have you read and liked? Do you hope that this book will appeal to a similar audience?

TR: You know, I haven't actually read any of those books, though I'm certainly aware of their existence. Trying to look at this novel objectively, I'd like to think it had something to do with two women who wrote extensively about the "domestic milieu," Ivy Compton-Burnett and Barbara Pym. Compton-Burnett showed the brute forces that really govern even the most apparently placid home life, and did it with such a deep wit that you feel like you're learning a new language. Pym takes what fiction had previously regarded as uninteresting material—the spinster's lot—and used it to give a beautifully acute and musical view of the paired-off world's romantic delusions.

But those are great writers. I'm not putting myself in their company. I do think looking at ordinary situations in a slightly crazy way—which is what I sense chick-lit novels do as well— can lead to a deeper insight than plodding, earnest, emotional explorations, however well intended. So in that sense our audiences might overlap, yes.

Q: Any chance we will meet Eve again—perhaps as a flourishing fashion designer, or as a frazzled mother of a hellion teenage girl (as she was once herself)?

TR: Eve is going to be a writer. On the last page of *Parallel Play* she is about to write the first page of her first novel. I would like to think she's a self-contained literary unit now. She's said all she has to say, through me. Besides, it's getting harder and harder to wriggle into this bra and panties.

Questions and Topics
for Discussion

1. What do you think Eve's name ("No last names in the Bible," as she explains) signifies in the context of *Parallel Play*?

2. Eve often seems extremely frustrated with motherhood—she even calls the infant Ann a "little bitch" in public. She can also be selfish and insensitive; her behavior after the death of Harvey's mother is particularly unfortunate. Is Eve a sympathetic character? Does Rayfiel succeed in humanizing Eve despite all her flaws? Would Eve make a good friend? If you disliked Eve, do you feel that her faults detracted from the book's merits?

3. Eve complains that she is a "useless" person and laments that "all [she] could do was copy" other people's dress designs. How does this observation apply to Eve's life in general? Is she the artist of her own life, or is she merely copying established roles and patterns? By the novel's end, has she regained some creative control over her life?

4. Though she often seems alone in her little world, many people (Harvey, Mark, Mindy, Alison, Marjorie) reach out to Eve

for her help and company, though not always with the best intentions. Is Eve lonely, or just dissatisfied?

5. How would you characterize the relationship between Eve and Harvey? What qualities that Eve possesses would attract a man of Harvey's personality? Can you imagine *Parallel Play* written from Harvey's point of view?

6. At one point in *Parallel Play*, Eve says of Harvey, "I loved him, by an act of will," but a few pages later, she says this of wearing clothes that she finds on the street: "It's about getting past the illusion of free will." But Eve is also exploited by others in ways that she doesn't "will," as when the film director uses her to manipulate an actress and when Mark grooms her to bear his wife's child. In what ways do marriage and motherhood compromise Eve's free will?

7. Is Mark a Machiavellian character? Is his behavior toward Eve sincere or coldly calculating?

8. Can *Parallel Play* be accurately characterized as "chick lit"? What do you think a male author brings to this novel's domestic, feminine milieu?

9. If you have read the previous novels in the author's Eve trilogy, *Colony Girl* and *Eve in the City*, what kind of profound changes—of behavior, temperament, outlook—do you think Eve shows after the events of three books? In what ways is she still the same person she was as a fifteen-year-old in Iowa?

10. Why do you think Rayfiel called the book *Parallel Play*?

PHOTO: © SIGRID ESTRADA

THOMAS RAYFIEL is the author of *Split-Levels; Colony Girl,* a *Los Angeles Times* Notable Book of the Year; and *Eve in the City.* He lives in Brooklyn, New York, with his wife, Claire, a potter, and their two children, Leo and Celia.